*Lungs
Full of
Noise*

The

Iowa

Short

Fiction

Award

In honor of James O. Freedman

University of

Iowa Press

Iowa City

Tessa Mellas

Lungs Full of Noise

University of Iowa Press, Iowa City 52242

Copyright © 2013 by Tessa Mellas

www.uiowapress.org

Printed in the United States of America

The University of Iowa Press is a member of Green Press
Initiative and is committed to preserving natural resources.

Printed on acid-free paper

ISBN-13: 978-1-60938-200-1
ISBN-10: 1-60938-200-5
LCCN: 2013934859

To my mother and father,

who encouraged me to make a life

of playing with words.

Contents

The Mariposa Club in the opening story is fictional and should not be taken as a representation of the esteemed Mariposa School of Figure Skating in Barrie, Ontario.

ACKNOWLEDGMENTS

I wish to extend my deepest gratitude to Jim McCoy, Allison T. Means, Charlotte M. Wright, Karen A. Copp, and all of the readers and editors at the University of Iowa Press who gave my manuscript such careful reads and who said yes to this rather strange bird of a book. Thanks also to freelance editor Will Tyler, freelance proofreader Judy Loeven, and fiction contest judge Julie Orringer. I will be forever appreciative and changed by this honor. Special thanks to the generous editors who first published stories from this collection and whose careful edits improved my work. I could never know all the names of the first readers and editorial assistants whose careful attention allowed my stories to first reach an audience, but I am grateful for your service.

I am grateful for the generosity and insight of my mentors: Barbara King from Kennedy School; Peter Bailey, Robert Cowser Jr., Mary Hussman, Natalia Singer, and Sid Sondergard at St. Lawrence; Lawrence Coates, Michael Czyzniejewski, and Wendell Mayo in Bowling Green; and Jim Braziel, Brock Clarke, Michael Griffith, Nicola Mason, Patrick O'Keeffe, and Leah Stewart in Cincinnati, who helped shape my aesthetic and these stories and whose writing, talent, and hard work have been inspirational.

For your friendship, insight, and support, special thanks to Derek Hall, Corey Murray, and Jenny Williamson at St. Lawrence; Sherita Armstrong-Guida, Mark Baumgartner, Karin Wraley Barbee and Matt Barbee, Jennifer Bryan, Jay Clevenger, Abigail Cloud, Lisa Crizer, Randy DeVita, Ashley Kaine, Byron Kanoti, Beth Kaufka, Rajni George, Alissia Linguar, Tasha Fouts Marren, Todd Marren, Beth Polzin, Kristin Poore, and Renee Reighart in Bowling Green; Becky Adnot-Haynes, Chelsea Bryant, Marjorie Celona, Lauren Clark, Mica Darley-Emerson, Megan Martin, Leah McCormack, Christine Muller-Held, Christian Moody, Daryl Osuch, David James Poissant, Hannah Rule, Ashlie Sandoval, B. R. Smith, Liv Stratman, Brian Trapp, Dietrik Vanderhill, Jessica Vozel, Suzanne Warren, Julia Wilcox, Ruth Williams, and Kathy Zlabek in Cincinnati; Christian Heiss and Jamie "P. J." Bordeau. Thank you to everyone else whose names I might have missed. So many people have influenced my life and writing but are too numerous to count or fit in these pages.

Love and thanks to my big fat Greek and Italian families, loud and colorful clans to which I am grateful to belong. Thanks especially to my mother-in-law and father-in-law Catherine Diltz and Richard McBride, who say that I am on par with Stephen King. To my grandmother, Helen Dokianos Mellas, whose shared love for books and bread will unite us always; I cannot imagine my life without you. To my sister, Elayna Hulett-Mellas, for sharing a childhood and many imaginative worlds. To Christ Mellas, a loyal and devoted father, whose work ethic and attention to detail are in me and in these stories. And to my mother, Celeste Ferrara Mellas, whose love for her daughters is infinite and without whose devotion and faith this book would not exist.

And finally to Matthew Diltz McBride, whose intelligence, patience, humor, and love have immensely enriched my life. Thank you for reading every word of this again and again. And thank you for sharing this eco-nutty, thrift-store, books-up-to-the-rafters adventure with me.

Grateful acknowledgment is made to the following publications in which these stories have appeared: "Mariposa Girls" in *Fugue*; "Bibi from Jupiter" in *StoryQuarterly*, reprinted in *Lightspeed Magazine* and in *The Lightspeed Year One Anthology*; "Blue Sky White" in *Hayden's Ferry Review* and reprinted in *Apocalypse Now: Poems and Prose from the End of Days*; "Landscapes in White" in *Washington Square Review*; "So Much Rain" in *Pank*; "Beanstalk" in *Crazyhorse*; "Six Sisters" in *Phoebe*; "So Many Wings" in *Prism International*; "Dye Job" in *The Collagist*; and "opal one, opal two" in Fifty-Two Stories' anthology *Forty-Stories: New Writing from Harper Perennial*. "Quiet Camp" is forthcoming in *The Pinch*.

Lungs
Full of
Noise

Mariposa
Girls

Last year, the girls wore dance skirts on the ice, sheer fabric tied at the waist, ribbons fluttering behind them—absurdly expressive tails. This year, they wear nothing. No skirts. No leotards. No tights. They skate naked, wind nipping their nipples, ice burn searing their thighs.

Along with their lycra, they gave up their skates, unscrewed the blades from the boots, and drilled them right into their feet. Two screws in the heel, three up front, secured into flesh and bone, just as one would mount them to wood. They say this way it's easier to point their toes in the air, to sink into the ice as the shock of descent shoots into their knees.

It all started with that girl with the ponytail pulled back so tight it distorted her eyes. Her double axel was shit, the landing an utter debacle. No one knew why. The setup was fine. Her legs scissored, and this motion propelled her body backward. She circled the ice in crisscrossing patterns, building up speed. An empty patch of ice would open. Her arms would pull back to fling limbs into rotation. A knee kicked up. Legs braided together. Ice passed below airborne feet. Then her toe would touch down, the blade sliding out from under her body, her tailbone hitting hard with a thud—falls that rattled the Plexiglas border and slapped her palms a startling pink.

Her coach said, "We've got to do something different if you're going to land that jump." What he meant was weight training or a different brand of boots. He didn't mean this.

But this is what she did. She shaved all the hair off her body, even the hair off her head. She took her father's drill from the tool shed, sterilized the screws, and lined the blades up on her feet. Then zip zip zip, she sent five screws into each foot and slipped skate guards over the blades. She went to bed bald and naked and in the morning showed up like this at the rink.

The first half hour on the ice, she seemed a bit shaky, probably the bones adjusting to the steel thread of the screws, her bare body getting used to the cold. She came off the ice flushed, her skin glistening wet from falling. Her coach slipped a coat over her shoulders, but she shrugged it away. She swallowed hungry gulps from the fountain, then went straight back out to the ice. By the twenty-fifth try she landed her double axel. Dwayne, the Zamboni man, said it was the most beautiful thing he had ever seen.

She landed fifteen more that day, perfectly cloned specimens, a jump she would never let go of again. Her body had memorized the precise vectors of speed and angle. They were engrained in her muscles, her bones, her skin.

She moved on from doubles to triples, as easily as a runner shifts from a jog to a run. She nailed them all, even the lutz. The arc of the landing was smooth and breathless, her leg stretching back in a stunning line from toe to chin. She stroked back and forth across the ice, sweeping into jumps that ascended above the boards. The mothers let out whoops from the stands, shouted, "Again! Again!" At that moment, she was all of their daughters, this beautiful creature who could do magnificent tricks.

By the end of the session, the other girls had stopped skating and stood by the boards to watch. They sipped silently from water bottles and wiped runny noses on the back of their gloves, bearing witness to a new breed of skater, a strange species—hairless and unconfined at the ankles, jumping higher and farther than ever before.

By the end of the month there were a dozen of them, boot-less girls with blades affixed to their feet, spinning quadruple and quintuple jumps never before seen. The other girls left, the ones who weren't willing to drill blades into their bones, who wanted to keep their hair, their skirts, their tights. Some went to other ice rinks. Some switched to ballet. Most moved on to other hobbies: to clarinets and pianos, to horseback riding and thespian club.

The ones who made it became skating prodigies overnight. They swept up medals across the country but were disqualified at Worlds. International judges vetoed their performances on the grounds of vulgar aesthetics. "This isn't the Garden of Eden," they said. "Sequins must adorn unmentionable parts."

By that time, the girls had started changing color. A dull gray spread through their fingers and toes, permanent frostbite setting in. The tips of their appendages were a deep dark purple, the skin fading as it went up their ankles and wrists.

"We'll just paint the rest of their bodies," the mothers said. "The way spandex clings, the judges will never know."

They hired artists to blend paint with the gray of the frostbite, spreading unitards across their daughters with blue and silver swirls. To finish the effect, they sewed sequins into their skin and dusted glitter over their heads. They were stunning, icicles stuck in their lashes, scalps shimmering blue. And so they went on win-ning the medals—while their fingers went numb and the tissue in their feet went dead.

Every so often one would disappear. There'd be whispers of am-putation, but no one spoke the word aloud. The Mariposa Club was a mecca of androgynous pixies. Every girl in America wanted to be a Mariposa Girl. They had seen them on TV. They knew Mariposa Girls were pretty. They knew Mariposa Girls always won. And so they were probably watching the night of the skating gala when one of the pixies fell.

It was a minute into her program. She had landed her quadruple axel but wobbled on the landing. She held on, but something wasn't right. Her blade was bent below her, loose and jiggling around. Still, she set up her quintuple loop, bent her knees for the takeoff, sprung into the air. For the longest moment, she floated, and the audience held their breath. When she came down, her ankle tipped sideways, and the screws sliced through her foot. She picked herself up and tried to keep going. But the flesh of her foot came open. There was nothing left to stand on, and she fell back against the ice. She lay there inert while the music played on. No one thought to stop the tape. They waited to hear her scream in pain. They waited to see the blood. But nothing spilled from her body. A wet shadow melted around her. Now she was nobody's daughter. Bald and naked, they could hardly tell who she was.

Bibi
from
Jupiter

When I marked on my roommate survey sheet that I'd be interested in living with an international student, I was thinking she'd take me to Switzerland for Christmas break or to Puerto Rico for a month in the summer. I wasn't thinking about a romp around the red eye of Jupiter, which is exactly what I'd have gotten had I followed my roommate home. Apparently, American school systems have gotten popular all over. Universities shepherd the foreigners in. Anything to be able to write on the brochures, "Our student body hails from thirty-three countries and the far reaches of the solar system."

You'd think there'd have been an uproar over the matter. I mean, here we have student funding going down the toilet and everyone staging protests to show they're pissed. And she gets a full ride, all the amenities paid for. She comes in like a Cuban refugee, minus the boat, sweeps up all the scholarships. And why shouldn't she? She probably qualifies as fifteen different types of minority. Don't get me wrong. I don't have anything against her. We were friends. I just didn't expect her to be so popular. I figured I'd have to protect her from riots and reporters. But as it turns out, she was really well liked.

The first time I met her I nearly peed my pants. It's the end of August and I've got all my stuff shoved in the family van, too unorganized for my father's taste, but we only live an hour away. I'm hoping to get there first to pick the best side of the room, the one with the most sunlight and least damaged furniture. I get up early—just to beat her there. But I don't.

She's sitting at her desk already, reading the student handbook. I double-check the room number: 317. I've got the right place. This is my roommate.

At first, I think she's an inmate. She's wearing this blue jump-suit. And she's got pale-green skin that looks sickly. Gangrene, I think, not quite knowing what that is. It just sounds like a disease that would turn you green. She's not an all-out green. Tinted rather, like she got a sunless tanner that didn't work out. Her ears are inset like a whale's, and she doesn't have eyelids. She's this tiny creature, not even five feet tall, completely flat, no breasts. It doesn't even look like she has nipples.

My parents are right behind me. My mother's carrying my lava lamp like some offering. My father's got my futon extended over his head, trying to be all macho in case my roommate's a babe. They drop my stuff on the side of the room with the broken closet door and turn to this green, earless girl. They're all excited, want to make friends with the new roommate. So they start asking questions: "How was your drive? Do you like the campus? Have your parents left?"

Not even acknowledging the obvious. That she's green. Maybe they didn't notice. Like I said, it was a pale green, a tint really, but it was pretty obvious to me, and she had weird eyes, beady black pinhead eyes like a hamster's.

So finally I ask, "Where are you from?"

And she says, "Jupiter."

"Jupiter, New York?" my parents ask.

Not that they know there *is* a Jupiter, New York. It just makes more sense than the other possibility.

"No," she says. "Jupiter, Jupiter. The planet."

"Oh," they say. "I didn't realize we'd found life on other planets yet. How interesting."

She says, "You didn't. We found you," and goes back to her reading.

That shuts my parents up fast. They have no response. They do an about-face and head back to the car.

"Jupiter," my father's saying. "You believe that, Cath?"

My mother's shaking her head, saying "Jupiter" over and over. First, like it's a word she's never heard, a word she's trying to get used to. Then like a question. "Jupiter?" Not quite sure whether to believe it. She says it several more times, looks at my father, then me.

"I was worried about Angela living with city kids," she says. "This is a bit different." She unlocks the car, grabs a handful of pillows, and adds, "Is Jupiter the one with the rings?"

"I thought Jupiter was made of gas," my father says. "How can she live on a gaseous planet?"

"Let's just drop it," I say. "She could be from the moon for all I care."

As it turned out, she *was* from the moon. Well, one of them. Apparently Jupiter's got a few dozen. The one she's from is called Europa—by Americans at least. But she tells everyone she's from Jupiter, says it's easier to explain. Her name is Bibi. No last name. Just Bibi. I looked it up. It means "lady" in Arabic. Ironic, as her kind doesn't have genders, just one type, like flowers, self-germinating and all. But she looks more like a girl than a guy, so that's how we treat her while she's here, even though her body parts serve both functions.

She tells me most of this the first night in the dorm. I'm unpacking my toiletries, and she's still reading. I say, "Your parents were cool with you coming to America? Mine wouldn't even let me go out of state."

"I don't have parents," Bibi says.

"Oh Christ!" I say. "I'm sorry. That sucks." What can you say in a situation like that? I'd never met an orphan.

"It's fine," she says. "Nobody has parents. I grew up like this, sort of in a dorm."

"How can nobody on Jupiter have parents?" I ask. I know I'm being nosy, but you've got to admit it's strange.

"It's complicated," she says. "I don't feel like getting into it."

I'm about to insist when there's a knock at the door. Bibi jumps to get it, and these men wheel in a full-size fridge. It's brand-new, a Frigidaire, one of those side-by-side freezer-and-fridge jobs complete with icemaker. They prop it against the window, plug it in, and leave.

"What the hell is that?" I ask, knowing damn well it's a fridge, not quite sure what it's doing in our room. My parents bought us one of those mini units, just enough space for a Brita filter, pudding snacks, and string cheese. The university had exact specifications on which ones were allowed. This Frigidaire's not on the list. Bibi explains how she got special permission to have it in the room, says she has a medical condition.

"What kind of condition?" I ask. "Are you contagious?"

"It's not a viral condition," she says. "I need a daily supply of ice."

"Ice," I say. "For what?"

"Don't they teach you this stuff in school?" she asks. "The basics of the solar system?"

"Of course," I say. "Third grade. We memorized the planets. There was a song."

Apparently she doesn't believe me. She goes to my dresser and starts grabbing stuff. She throws my nightie in a lump in the middle of the floor, says, "That's the sun." She places a red thong beside it and calls that Mercury. Venus is a pair of toe socks. Earth a blue bra. Mars a pair of leggings. And Jupiter and all its moons are my best sparkly panties. She lines them up, stands to the side, says, "See?"

"Yeah, I get your point," I say, though I don't really. I'm too pissed that my underwear are on the floor. Matching bras and panties aren't cheap. "I appreciate the astronomy lesson," I say, but she cuts me off.

She points at my bra. "You're here," she says. "We're there. See how far we are from the sun? It's cold. We don't have sweat glands. Your planet is hot, so I need ice. Capisce?"

Capisce? Who the hell does she think she is? A Jupiterian girl trying to intimidate me with Italian. Barging in with her refrigerator. Taking the best side of the room and making my thong a planet. I snatch her solar system off the floor and stuff it back in my drawer, say, "I don't know much about Jupiter, but here, shit like that isn't cool."

There's another knock at the door. I'm about to say, "That better not be a stove," when these guys from down the hall walk in. They want Bibi to join them for a game of pool.

"I'm Angela," I say, extending my hand.

"You can come too if you want," they say. But it's clear they're just interested in Bibi.

I shrug. "I got stuff to do. Maybe next time."

And Bibi takes off. No apology. No, "I'm not going without my roommate." No nothing. She just leaves me there with her big fucking fridge while she goes to shoot pool with these boys she's never even seen. I'm not sure what they see in her. She isn't at all pretty. I mean, I don't think so. We have rigid aesthetics here, right? How can you count a green earless girl without eyelids as pretty?

I watch them head down the stairs. The dorm is quiet, empty. I thought people were supposed to congregate on their floor the first night, praise each other's bedspreads and posters and shit. The door across the hall opens and a guy wearing pink pants and a polo shirt steps out.

"Hey," I say.

"Hey," he replies.

He's wearing his collar propped up like he's Snow White. His hair is gelled back and goopy. I want to tell him that went out of style with the Fonz, but instead say, "I'm Angela," even though it's written on the construction paper sign on my door.

"Call me Skippy," he says, even though his sign says John Ward III.

"Where'd the nickname come from?" I ask.

"I made it up. People say you can reinvent yourself in college."

"Huh," I say. "Good choice."

"So that green girl's your roommate?" he asks.

"Yeah. Afraid so."

"Do you know when she's getting back?" he asks. "I heard she's from Jupiter. You think you could introduce me? *Lloyd in Space* is my favorite cartoon."

The first week wasn't at all what I expected from freshman year. Bibi followed me all over the place, dragging her leaky ice packs along. Didn't quite understand that we had different schedules. She's taking all these science and math courses. And I have this good mix. Swahili. Ballet. Psychology. Statistics. My adviser made me take that last one, said I needed a math credit. But besides statistics, I'm thinking classes should be fun.

Then in psych lab, I turn around and there she is. She's even got the books. I figure she must have bought them for both our schedules. How's a girl from Jupiter to know better?

Everyone wants to be her lab partner. They crowd around her desk and ask stupid questions like, "Are you going to be a psychologist? Will you go back to Jupiter and counsel manic-depressives?"

"No," she says. "I'm a neurobiology major. Stem cell research. I'm going to learn how to grow pancreases and livers on rats, then take them back to Jupiter and implant them in bodies."

"Right," I say. "You're not even supposed to be here. Don't you have chemistry?"

She doesn't answer, just prepares her rat for the maze.

Of course, hers finishes first. Mine gets stuck in a corner and goes into shock.

But what does it matter that her rat's the smartest. The girl doesn't have common sense. She forgets her shoes all the time, puts the toothpaste in her mouth instead of on the brush, and doesn't close the stall door when she goes to the bathroom. No one wants to see how Jupiterians pee. Actually, everyone was interested, but once they saw it, they didn't want to see it again.

Around the third week I finally get a look at her schedule. It's in one of those ugly-ass Trapper Keeper things. As it turns out, Bibi *is* enrolled in my classes. Hers too. She's taking nine at once. I didn't think that was allowed. They must make exceptions for Jupiterians, figuring anyone from another planet is more intelligent than us. Bibi is pretty smart actually, gets perfect scores on the tests even though she says absolutely nothing in class.

And to top it all off, the boys are into her too. That guy Skippy won't stop hanging around. He's a complete dork, a Grade-A loser. He stands outside our door like he's the king's guard. At night he brings Bibi ice cream and Popsicles. He follows her to dinner and leaves flowers outside our door, nasty weedy ones with ants. Bibi hangs them from the ceiling, and the flowers die because there's no light in the room. She won't let me open the blinds, not even a crack, on account of her condition. So now we've got all these ants crawling across our ceiling between brown crusty root systems. And Skippy's become this stalker. I find him in my closet behind my shoe rack and Dustbuster.

"Just playing hide-and-seek," he says, and winks.

"Hide-and-seek, my ass," I yell. "She doesn't even have a vagina!"

I call my mother and tell her about Skippy and the ice packs and the ants. My mother tells me to be patient. She reminds me about Martin Luther King Jr. I tell her she shouldn't send Bibi presents anymore. She puts something in all my care packages for Bibi. Cookies. Statuettes from the dollar store. *Soup-for-the-Soul* books. I tell her, "Bibi doesn't need presents. You should see this girl's checks. The government gives her plenty of money."

My mother says presents are different. Bibi doesn't have parents. She tells me to be mindful of that. I tell my mother no one on Jupiter has parents. She says that doesn't sound right, and I agree. I mean a whole planet full of orphans. That just seems too sad to be true. She's probably lying. Going for the sympathy vote. I could press the issue, but I don't. I think about Martin Luther King Jr., and when Bibi comes back, I give the roommate chitchat thing another try.

"So who do you have the hots for?" I ask.

And she says, "Nobody really."

I'm not quite sure how it works for Jupiterians, since they can self-germinate. She seems asexual. She never mentions boys.

I say, "What about Skippy? He wants you bad."

"Oh him," she says, as though she hadn't noticed. She gets her shower caddy and heads down the hall.

Maybe she's bisexual. Maybe she's gay. I wonder if she masturbates when I'm out of the room. It seems like genderless people don't care about anyone but themselves. They might, but Bibi could give two shits about me.

By the time Thanksgiving rolls around, I'm getting pretty sick of my roommate. I mean how many times do you have to tell a person, "Put on your shoes," before she gets it? There's snow on the ground, and she's prancing around in it like some leprechaun. Her bare feet leave monster frog prints. Did I mention Jupiterians only have three toes? It's like she needed to show them off. You'd think she at least would have tried to fit in. I think she liked being different. Everyone was always stopping by our room to see what the space alien was up to. I was happy to have a week at home without her.

But there was no place for her to go, and my mother offered our house, insisted really, said, "Angela, if we were dead, I would hope someone would be nice enough to take you in for the holidays."

I guess she was right. Bibi couldn't very well go back to the moon. The least I could do was share my goddamn turkey with the girl. My turkey. My gravy. My family.

Bibi stayed in the guest room, and wouldn't you know it, she gets along great with my mom. Better than me. The two of them bonded like bears.

My mother showed her how to cook cranberry sauce and corn bread from scratch and, of course, how to pull the guts out of a turkey. Bibi was fascinated, watched my mother tear the bird's insides out of its ass, leaving the middle hollow and pink. Bibi couldn't stop staring at it, until finally I said, "It's only a turkey. Gobble, gobble."

Bibi didn't answer, just looked at me like I'd threatened to cut off her head.

And my mother said, "Angela, why don't you help your father clean the garage?"

Things went on like this for days, my mother acting like Bibi's her new adopted daughter and treating me like chopped meat.

Then Thanksgiving Day, we sit down for dinner and, of course, my mother makes us hold hands. We do this every year, even though we're a family that doesn't go to church. Even though we're a family that doesn't pray. My mother insists we believe in God.

She starts out as usual with, "Thank you, Lord, for the food before us." Then she goes off on this new part, says, "Thank you for bringing this space child into our lives. May our civilizations be as peaceful as those of the Pilgrims and Indians."

I want to say, "God, Mom, does everything have to be about Bibi?" Instead, I grab the nicest piece of turkey and dump gravy all over, a little extra in case Bibi helps herself to more than her fair share. But she doesn't. She takes some potatoes and squash, a little cranberry sauce and corn bread, really small portions. My father tries to pass her the turkey.

"Don't you like meat?" he asks.

My mother says, "Bill, maybe she's vegetarian."

"No," Bibi says. "It's just that the turkey reminds me of my mother."

I want to ask Bibi what the hell she meant at dinner, but she goes to bed early and shuts the door. The next day my mother takes us to the mall. I'm thinking she feels bad about the turkey thing because she tells us to buy any outfit we want. But Bibi doesn't want clothes. She goes to the cooking store and buys a turkey baster. And now I'm really confused.

We go to the food court for lunch. We get Sbarro's, chow mein, and Arby's. My mom's sucking a slushie. She gives Bibi a sip, says, "Tell me about your mother."

Bibi says, "I never had a mother. No one does. She died before I was born."

It's been three months and this chick still hasn't explained the no-parents situation. So I say, "What's the deal? No parents. No fathers. How exactly do you make babies?"

My mother gives me this look like I'm being rude.

"What?" I say. "You started it."

Bibi swallows the rest of her egg roll, asks, "You wanna see?"

"What? Here?" my mother says.

She lifts her shirt, and there's this hole where her belly button should be. It's the size of a nickel, but it scoops in and up like a funnel. She does this right in the middle of the food court. People turn and stare. My mother tells her to pull down her shirt.

"So it's like a vagina," I say.

"Except you put your own pollen up there, push it in deep instead of flushing it."

"What a relief," my mother says. "I thought you couldn't have children."

"I can," Bibi says. "But I won't. Anyone who has a baby ends up dead."

"Childbirth used to be risky here," my mother says. "Thank God for modern medicine."

"No," Bibi says. "Procreation is suicide. Babies can't come out the bottom. There's no hole. In birth, they gnaw through your stomach. They eat your organs on the way out."

I sit there, shocked, my fries turning to mush on my tongue. "My God," I say. "Why would anyone want to get pregnant?"

"They say it's wonderful. Like being on heroin for nine months. The best euphoria there is."

"Christ Almighty," I say, "that's some mad kind of population control." I ask her if she's heard of the one-child law in China, but she doesn't answer.

"You're in good hands now," my mother says and gives her a hug, rocks her back and forth in her arms. Right there in the middle of the food court like she's five years old. I just sit and stare at my food. As though I could eat after that.

My mother drops us off at school on Sunday, tells Bibi if she needs anything to call. We carry our laundry upstairs. Under our folded clothes, we find notes from my mother on matching stationery taped to bags of Hershey's kisses. Mine says, "Loved having you home. So nice to spend time with you and Bibi."

"Your mom's really cool," Bibi says. She props her turkey baster and note on her dresser.

"Yeah," I say. "I guess."

Now that she likes my mom, she wants to be friends with me. Go figure.

I curl up on my futon with a piece of leftover corn bread. "So did you ever think of doing it?" I ask. "Just to see what pregnancy's like? Don't you think you will eventually?"

"Why would I do that?" she says.

"Don't you think you're missing out? You said it's like drugs. I'd try that."

"I don't want to die," Bibi says. "That's why I'm here."

"How does your planet feel about stem cell research?" I ask.

"They don't understand why things should change."

"Yeah, it's kind of the same in America," I say. "Stem cell research is a sin. Better watch out. They might throw you out of the country."

She empties her chocolate kisses into the porcelain bowl my mother gave her.

"I think you'll do it," I say. "That's what the turkey baster's for, right? To stick the pollen all the way up?"

She stares at me with her black eyes bugging out, and for a second I think she's going to throw the bowl at my head. Either that or she's going to cry. But she just walks out of the room.

She didn't come back that night. I wasn't sure where she went. And frankly, I couldn't care less.

―――――――

Bibi didn't speak to me for weeks. We gave each other the silent treatment and kept slamming doors. I called my mother and told her I wanted to switch rooms. She said, "Angela, that's not how we deal with our problems."

I went to the RA and asked how long it would take to get a new room. She said I could file a complaint, but room changes were rarely approved.

It looked like Bibi and I were stuck with each other, at least for six more months. I started thinking I should muster up some sort of reconciliation. I thought about apologizing. Maybe she'd apologize for being such a bitch. I had a plan, was going to do it after my last class the Monday before finals. I swear I was going to.

But then I get back to my room, and Bibi's in bed with Skippy. He's straddling her stomach. His schlong's way up in her belly, shoved in there real good. He's riding her like a madman, and Bibi's arching up so her belly keeps hitting his balls.

I slammed the door behind me and slept in the lounge.

Who did she think she was having sex with a human boy, and one from our floor? It's not that I liked him. He was too pimply for me. But she'd been lying to me all semester, pretending she didn't understand my crushes, and now this. She loses her virginity to Skippy. She loses her virginity first. I couldn't believe a Jupiterian had beaten me to it.

Still, I figured I'd be the bigger person. I figured we should talk. The next day, I get back from ballet, and she's sitting at her desk reading chemistry, taking pages of notes, pretending like nothing happened. So I sit on my futon and sigh this huge sigh, hoping she'll get the gist we need to talk. And when that doesn't work, I say, "If you're going to be one of those kinds of girls, we need a system."

She says, "Skippy told me to put a bra on the door. I don't have any. Is that what you mean?"

"Yeah, that's what I mean," I say. And then, "So what's the big idea? I thought you were genderless. Were you lying about the self-germination?"

"I can't get pregnant the human way. It's got to be my own pollen. You're not even the right species."

"A girl who can't get pregnant," I say. "The boys are going to love that."

She shrugs. She doesn't even care that she just lost her cherry. It doesn't even faze her.

"So did you orgasm all over good ole Skippy?" I ask. "Was he good? Can Jupiterians even get off?"

"You're so stupid," she says. "Would a species survive if they couldn't orgasm?"

"Screw you," I say. I grab my towel and shower caddy and slam the door behind me. Emily, our next-door neighbor, is just leaving for class.

"God," I say, "that Bibi is such a whore. I wish she'd warn me before she fucks guys in the room."

Emily says, "Really? Bibi? I didn't know she could. We were all wondering about that."

"Yeah," I say. "She's a little bitch."

"Didn't she go to your house?" Emily says. "I thought you were friends."

"Not anymore."

I pound down the hall as loud as I can, though flip-flops don't make much noise. I slam the bathroom door to let the whole floor know Bibi's a skank. I let the hot water wash over my back. "Slut," I say under my breath. And then a little louder, "At least I'm not a slut." I say it as though I'm talking to someone in the opposite shower stall. "You're such a slut." I imagine Bibi across from me. I say it once more, almost shout it, "You're the biggest slut in the galaxy, and I wish you'd go back to the moon!"

I'm not sure if it was Skippy who spread the word or Emily. It might even have been me, proclaiming loudly from the shower that day. Whoever it was, my bra ended up on the door an awful lot the next month. I left a note on her desk that said, "Stay the hell away from my underwear drawer."

Bibi did a different guy nearly every day. I saw one of those little black books on her desk. She had all the boys on the hall penciled in. There were even names I didn't know. She really *had* turned into a whore. I wondered if they paid her or if she did it for free. I missed the old Bibi. The Bibi who forgot her shoes. The Bibi who studied all night. The Bibi who didn't know shit about boys.

We didn't talk anymore. We just came and went as though we didn't know each other. I moved my futon into Emily's room and slept there most nights. I wondered what would become of Bibi. I figured her grades would plummet, and she'd get kicked out of school. But when I got back from Christmas break, her marks were posted on the wall, nine A's. She'd completed a whole year of college in four months.

I'm not sure how she kept it up, the sex and the studies. Second semester, she upped her course load to ten. They even let her into a graduate class. Like I said, if you're not from America, they let you get away with that shit.

Then around February she starts looking greener. I wonder if she has that seasonal depression thing. Then one day, I get back to my room, and Bibi's jumping all over her bed. She's got the music cranked as high as it goes, some god-awful Broadway crap, and she's singing, "I feel pretty. Oh so pretty." And she's wearing this outfit that's half her clothes and half mine with my sparkly panties around her head.

"What the hell's going on?" I say. "I thought I told you not to touch my stuff."

She jumps off her bed and dances this little jig. And she looks so goddamn ridiculous I have to laugh.

"Did you find some solution to Jupiter's baby problem?" I ask. "Is your research going well?"

"No," she says. "I'm pregnant."

"You're not," I say. "I thought you couldn't."

"Well, it's not like I had proof it was impossible," she says. "I guess it is. I'm pregnant with a half-human baby." At this, she bursts out laughing. Pollen puffs out her ears in yellow clouds.

"Who?" I say. "Whose baby is it?"

"A boy's," she says. "A human boy's." Then she's surrounded by pollen again. She swirls it around with her hands. "Can you believe that?"

"Are you going to keep it?" I say. "If you give birth, it'll kill you, right?"

"I'm giving birth to the first half-human, half-Jupiterian baby ever!" she screams. She rips the panties off her head and twirls them in the air.

"Can't you get an abortion? Those are common here. They'll get rid of it. You'll be fine."

"I don't want an abortion," she says. "I want to be eaten alive."

I didn't know what to say. She'd turned ten types of crazy. It must have been that euphoria she told me about. I began to wish

I had a normal human roommate I could take to the abortion clinic so things would be better. I'd never had a friend with a life-threatening illness. Only grandfathers and uncles. And all of them died. There was nothing I could do. Bibi had lost it. Her condition was terminal, and she was ecstatic, fucking over the moon.

In the weeks that followed, Bibi stopped seeing the boys. I moved my futon back to our room, and we started talking again. I became Bibi's bodyguard, shielding her from all the male scum on the floor. Boys would stop by and say, "I'm here for some alien sex."

I'd say, "Fuck off, asshole." And they'd go away.

By March, Bibi had given up her studies. No more stem cell research. Instead, she holes herself up in our room making sculptures out of dining hall silverware. She hangs them from the ceiling where the ants used to be and opens the windows to watch them blow in the breeze.

We start having parties in our room every weekend. People bring beer and fill up our fridge. The RA doesn't give a damn because Bibi got her through chemistry first semester, and she hopes she'll get her through physics next fall.

I call my mother and tell her we're getting along great. I tell her Bibi is the best. My mother's glad we're back to being friends, says she knew we'd work it out. I don't mention that Bibi is pregnant. My mother would be disappointed. She wouldn't understand.

Finally, Bibi and I do everything together like roommates should. We order pizza at midnight, rate the guys on the hall, re-decorate the room. We move the beds against one wall and scatter huge pillows on the floor. Bibi finds these red Christmas lights on sale at the hardware store and hangs them up. She turns them on and lies under her swaying spoons, pretends she's watching hot liquid hydrogen swirl around Jupiter from the moon. She says, "Angela, come lie with me. We can watch Jupiter together. Better enjoy me while you can. Pretty soon, this baby will eat its way out."

"Don't talk like that," I say.

"Like what?" She dangles her three-toed feet in the air, says, "It's okay. It's only death."

―――――――

By April she's really showing. She's got this great green hump of a belly, draws faces on it with finger paint and calls it Skippy Junior. Every day she plans something different. She says, "Let's take Skippy Junior to the zoo. Let's take Skippy Junior ice skating. Let's take Skippy Junior for parachute lessons."

I say, "Bibi, I've got classes."

She says, "I'm going to be dead in a few months. You can study then."

So we go ice skating and snorkeling and rent lots of porno and drink slushies. Bibi does this thing with her turkey baster, fills it up with slushie and lets it volcano into her mouth. Half goes in. Half gets all over, which makes the ants come back. But this is kind of great, just like before when we hated each other, and Skippy was a stalker. Back when Bibi studied all the time and didn't care about parties or drinking or boys.

The new Bibi is completely different. She dances all over the room, begs me to go to clubs, says, "You gotta teach me that booty bounce thing." She puts on a sparkly shirt and lipstick, a short skirt and heels. She tapes a paper bow tie to her stomach and says, "Skippy Junior's ready."

So that's what we do. We go to the only dance club in town, Freaky Willy's. And I teach her to dance the American way. I show her how to grind like a skanky ho.

We run into Skippy at the club. He's there with some guys. His acne looks a bit better. He buys us drinks, Coronas all around. You've got to give him credit. At least he got us good beer. Then he wants to dance with Bibi. He seems genuine enough. Anyhow, there's no way he can get sex with her funnel closed up. One of those really bouncy songs comes on with the flashing lights, and Bibi drags Skippy to the dance floor and rocks it out.

I sit at the bar and watch. She's picked up the booty bounce, no problem. She looks kind of sexy gyrating her tiny hips, her shoulders bopping with the music. In this light, she doesn't even look green. Skippy puts his hand on her back and tries to shake his pelvis too. But you can tell he's not the dancing type.

Later, he walks us home, and Bibi invites him in. I go to Emily's room for a bit.

When he's gone, I ask, "So does he want you back? Is it his baby?"

"It's nobody's baby," she says. "On Jupiter, no one belongs to anyone else."

That was the last time I saw Bibi. When I woke up, she was gone. There was a note on my desk that said, "Thanks for teaching me to dance. Thanks for sharing your family." Most of her stuff was still there. I assume she went back to Jupiter, but who's to be sure. I don't like to think of other possibilities.

After that, there were lots of policemen and school officials who wanted to know where she went. I told them I didn't know. Word got out to the papers. Skippy came by our room and put a bouquet of weedy flowers by the door.

He said, "I really loved her. I don't know why she had sex with all those guys."

"I know," I said. "I'm sure it was your baby."

I invited him in. We sat on Bibi's bed real close, and it felt better, that warmth, being next to someone who understood. We stayed like that for hours, shoulder to shoulder, not even talking. When it got dark, we slid under the covers. I was wearing those sparkly panties, the ones Bibi tossed on the floor that first night, the ones that were Jupiter. Skippy slid his hand down the front, brushed his fingers against what I imagined to be Bibi's moon. I didn't even mind when he aimed his boner at my belly button. I guided it lower, and he found the right hole.

"What if she comes back?" he asked.

"She's gone," I said, and kissed him hard.

He moved his hips back and forth and buried his head in my neck. My eyes locked on the turkey baster on Bibi's dresser, and I tried to imagine that she had never been here. That she had never existed. That I had gotten here all on my own.

Blue
Sky
White

─────────────

The first day the sky is white, nobody is suspicious. Every so often this happens. The sky drains of color and fills with fog, blanched white like porous bone. A transient member of the landscape, the white hovers mute, distant as the moon. We expect the blue back shortly, so we treat the white like a visitor who never stays long. The children hope it will postpone a departure. While it is here, they draw pictures with frantic fury, saving their blue crayons for oceans and eyes. While the sky is white, their drawings require less effort. They leave the top of the page uncolored. For now, a blank background is accurate enough.

The second day the sky is white, the mothers set jugs and dish tubs out on the hardened dirt of the front yards. No need to haul water from the creek. Rain will wash over rooftops and spill over eaves into bottles and buckets and bowls. The sky will deliver it to our doorsteps. As in the time of the great irrigation ditches, the grandfathers say. The children sit cross-legged and listen, knees bent like the points of a star. The grandfathers tell how water once traveled from a faraway mountain to the town where we live, coursing through cuts in the ground. And when it arrived, it trickled into the house through a hollow groove carved under the wall, like a winged creature that folds itself up and slips through the sliver of space between door and ground.

In the second week of whiteness, the maple tree at the center of town drops all its seedpods on the very same day instead of gradually as when the sky was blue. They twirl and tumble, traverse a spiraled path through the air, cover the ground with a tan carpet of miniature tails. The grandmothers think the sky has stored up rain for a deluge, to soften the earth, to loosen layers, making a habitable home for roots. They say now that the sky is white, forests could surround us again. Our descendents could have wood for fires, wood for rooftops, wood to carve into boxes and toys and flutes. And if they use the trees sparingly, in a hundred years they will be able to count the layers of rings, tracing back to this day, this year. To find out when the sky gave up its color, forfeiting cerulean landscapes for the company of treetops and birds.

The grandfathers say nothing but a factory could turn the sky so suddenly white. So, after a third week of whiteness, the fathers depart to see if the factory has opened again. It has been generations since anyone worked there. Still the stories live on. Stories of smoke pouring from chimneys, fire sparking behind panes of glass. Of metal parts churning and grinding, like teeth gnawing the sinews of flesh to pulp. A mechanical mastication, rhythmic, sonorous—the fathers say they sense it in their sleep—an inheritance from ancestors who lived and worked at the factory, for months away from home, until the day the factory shut down, and the fathers were sent away. They carried the factory home in pieces. Cogs and spindles in their pockets. Wrenches, grates, and rails in their packs. These things are still on our mantles. The fathers polish them before they leave. They pack quickly and depart in the morning, burlap bags filled with bread and water and roots. A huddled mass of bodies and packs, they seem like a small mountain moving away.

Before the sky lost its color, half the children in town had blue eyes, and the others had hazel or brown. Nobody thought much of this difference until the blue relinquished its post in the sky. Now the blue-eyed children are better than those with eyes the color of grass or ground. Their mothers give them more meal in the morning, spend more time brushing and braiding their hair at night. And when they tuck their blue-eyed children into bed, they say, Don't close your eyes quite yet. They move close, stare hard, try to lose themselves in the sapphire pools that circle the darks of their eyes.

When the sky stays white for the fourth week in a row, the grand-mothers look for signs that the blue is coming back. They stand outside with their chins tipped up, their long gray braids trail-ing behind them, marking the ground with indentations like the footprints sparrows once left in the yards. They stare like that for hours, trying to separate sky from cloud. They wonder if the sky is all cloud. Or perhaps a cloudless albino, stripped of pigment and sight. They search for any vague hint. A splotch of color. A wave of blue. A dot like a star in the morning sky. Every day, one of the grandmothers thinks she sees it. She points and yells for us to come. There. Look, she says. See? The blue's coming back. But there is never a hint of color. Nothing but white over infinite white.

The fathers head westward at a giddy pace toward the white hori-zon that seems every day whiter the farther they get from their families, the closer they come to the edge of the world. They keep going through the early hours of darkness and rest when they no longer can see. At night their legs ache, the ligaments in their calves tender from the stretch of long-legged strides. They compare pains. They argue over whose bones carry more weight. They hold on to their hurt, let it linger. They savor the tight twisting of muscles, relish the sweet satisfaction of tired limbs.

A week after the fathers leave, a baby is born with skin that is white rather than the tawny color of flesh. When his mother holds him up to the sky, he nearly disappears. His skin is covered with blue veins. Gnarls of them weave their way from his thumbs to his neck. More run across his legs and chest like rivers meandering across dry sand. He is like a map, the mothers say. They wonder if they follow the lines on his body, will they come to a place where the sky is still blue? The mothers take turns holding him. They make soft sounds and stroke his skin with their lips, hoping the blue will spread like ink, wetting their tongues, their throats, their insides. Filling them with something like wonder, soaking their cells in bliss.

Gradually, the blue of the blue-eyed children dissolves into a pale gray the color of stone. Like the blue in the sky, the color seeps out slowly, fading as though soaked in sun. The mothers glare at their children, imagine them harboring the blue inside, under the white crescent moons of their fingers, caged in the spaces between their ribs. The mothers rush through bedtime stories, let their daughters weave their own braids. At night, they are eager for the flutter of lids closing down over colorless eyes. They hope the night will be long, the darkness more desirable than the bare white of morning or the ash of afternoon.

More and more often the mothers send their children to the town landfill, though there has been no waste to dump for years. The mothers tell the children to look for things of color. To search for something blue. The children dig through the ground and tear back rocks, ripping through layers of human things. These days they must dig deep to find anything at all. A knick-knack, a stub of crayon, beads a long time loose of their thread. They sift through shards of bottles and dishes. They stack tin cans and plastic lids. They pocket small pieces of metal and pretend they understand the use of these things. Metal molded into odd shapes, into brackets and knobs and angles, into coils and rods and springs. At home, they arrange them on the floorboards, trying to find parts that fit together, that belonged to the same machine that sat on somebody's table and made music or food or heat.

When the baby with the world's waterways on its skin turns one month old, another change arrives. The maple tree at the center of town turns a startling red. The mothers and children rush inside. Red is not a color that generally brings good. But the grandmothers know better. It is foliage, they say. They explain the seasons. The children ask if the tree must really lose its leaves. The grandmothers say, Yes, the tree must give them up so the snow knows when to fall. The children ask them to describe snow, and the grandmothers tell them it is the brightest form of white. But the sky is white already, the children say. Of course, the grandmothers answer, then the opposite will occur. When the blue in the sky turns white, the white in the snow turns blue.

When the fathers arrive at the factory, they find that nothing has changed. The doors are still bolted shut on rusty hinges, the windows blocked by corrugated metal sheets. They circle the building until they find a piece of metal loose enough to peel back; then they rip and pull 'till it's free. They take turns peering in through the corner of a window but see only white sky reflected in glass. So they smash out the glass in the panel and brush away pieces shiny with blood. They take turns touching the air inside, wondering what it would be like to exist in this building. The thunder of mechanization comes alive in their hands.

The grandfathers tell the children about a land on the other side of the world where everything is exactly the opposite of how it is here. They tell the children they can dig a hole straight down to get there—for miles and miles, for years and years. It will be a very dark tunnel, the grandfathers say. You will have to crawl on your hands and knees. But when you emerge on the other side, you will find the blue sky above you again. They are holding it hostage. You must go and teach these people to share. We will start the hole in the landfill where the soil is already loose. We will work in shifts. We will dig with the claws of our hands.

The mothers knew the fathers would be gone at least a month. They knew they would wake to empty beds. But they did not agree to six weeks of whiteness. They wake in the early hours of morning to see if the sky has changed. But it is the same morning over and over. They close the curtains and wander through their homes, opening cupboards and drawers, pulling back floorboards, rubbing dirt on the white of the walls. Anything to distract themselves from the hollow sky. Anything to pass the empty hours of day. They flip through faded books from their closets, brittle, falling apart. There is no one left who reads this language, but the mothers are only interested in the maps. Maps of towns with houses. Maps of mountain ranges and railway tracks. They look for the symbols that mean water. That mean lakes and oceans and rivers, expanses of blue spread over blue.

The grandmothers used to bake bread. They used to weave and sweep and dig for roots. But they gave up these things when the tree turned red. They set up station under its branches so they could keep a closer watch on the sky. They remind the sky of winter. They remind the sky of snow. When the children gather around to watch, the grandmothers say, You'll see. The snow will come. Blue snow. And the land will look like the ocean floor. The children ask again about the ocean. The grandmothers talk about mermaids and whales. They say, The sky will realize its error when the blue snow falls to the ground. Then will they trade? the children ask. The grandmothers say, Yes, they will barter for each other's clothes.

On the day the dig to the other side of the world begins, a child finds a vase in the dump. A bright colored vase. A vase that might be blue. Look, the child says running through town with the item clutched in her hand. I found it. I found blue. I brought it back. That's not blue, the grandmothers say. It's purple. The mothers think it's green. They bring the vase to the house with the baby and hold it up to the veins on its chest. It doesn't match, the mothers say. The children ask, If it's not blue, then what color is it? The mothers say, It's a color that doesn't exist. They are about to send the children away when one of them notices a spot on the baby's leg. A birthmark, the mothers tell her. It's the same red as the tree, the child says.

After weeks of staring into the sky, one of the grandmothers goes blind. They realize too late what has happened. The sky is too bright for the naked eye. Snow blindness, they call it. They say no one must go outside. Or all will be blinded by whiteness. They must protect their eyes. So they close the shutters and hang blankets over the walls. When they venture out for water, they cover their heads with veils so the only direction they can see is down. They find their way to the creek by watching the pattern of pebbles change underfoot. The children are only allowed out with their mothers. They sit sullen inside and draw pictures with the last stubs of black and brown crayons. No more pretty colors. Used up. Rubbed away. No more left at the dump. They draw silhouettes of their mothers, shading the eye sockets darker and darker, tracing the soft clefts of their lips.

Each night when the rest of the town is sleeping, the children sneak from their beds. They convene at the town landfill to continue their work on the hole. Now the hole is the diameter of a bedroom, almost two stories deep. The children clear bucket after bucket of dirt, passed up to the grandfathers on ropes. They scrape at the ground with their fingers. They weasel stones and objects out with their toes. They stop when the sky softens to the blurry gray of dawn, their skin salty with perspiration, their hearts pounding against agile frames. They look up the steep sides of the tunnel at the circle of white brightening overhead. Too tired to climb out, they lie back on the ground, heel to heel, and hand to hand. Letting the cool soil slow their heartbeats. Letting the sky's whiteness wash over their skin.

When the houses fall silent, the mothers creep outside and congregate around the tree, whose crimson leaves are falling, leaving bare limbs to hold up the sky. They are certain the red spot on the baby's leg is a landmark showing them where to start. They will take the baby and follow the map until they find the blue again. They cannot endure this town any longer, a town with an obstinate sky. It isn't stealing exactly, they say. We have every intention of bringing him back. They say, We would never take a baby. Except for the good of the town.

As the mothers head east with the baby, the fathers appear from the west within sight of a tree stripped bald and naked, but for a few brown leaves clinging still. The tree has turned into a skeleton, spidery limbs scratching the sky. The fathers wonder if they came in the right direction. They retrace their steps in their heads. Perhaps they veered off course. Perhaps they have arrived in a different town. They consider the people who might inhabit these houses. Children who are not their children. Women who are not their wives.

When the grandmothers awaken, the houses are silent except the low whisper of wind over the roofs. They amble from room to room, feeling in all the dark corners for children tucked in shadows, stifling giggles with hands pressed to their lips. The grandmothers listen for the rise and fall of breathing. They listen for the shuffle of shoes. Though it is dark, they sense that the rooms are empty. They wonder what has happened now. Maybe the white is blotting out the people, or the sky has soaked them up. Then they hear a sharp knock outside. They hear footsteps dashing from door to door. A mother without proper covering to protect her eyes. Searching for a baby covered in blue rivers with a red tree marked on its thigh.

The children try to climb out of the hole, but the walls are too steep, their arms and legs fatigued. So they keep digging. They want to reach the other side of the world before the fathers return. They rip into the ground with their fingers, scraping out dirt with hands cupped like spades. They lose track of the opening above them and fall into a rhythm, burrowing farther and farther down. They don't realize when the dirt gets wet, when their knees sink down in mud. They carve into the water table. They tunnel into the ocean floor.

Nobody is home but the grandmothers when the fathers push open the doors. The grandmothers shrink back from the sudden light and shield their eyes. The fathers say, It's only us. The grandmothers cry, Oh, thank god you're here. They explain how they awoke with everyone gone. They say no one should be outside. On account of the blindness that came when the leaves turned red. On account of the white of the snow. The fathers try to calm them, but then the grandfathers arrive. They are breathless with elation. They are hiccupping for joy. Come quick, they say. The children did it. They've swum to the other side of the world. They show them the hole in the landfill, a tunnel with no end. The fathers tie ropes around their waists and the grandfathers lower them down. The fathers descend hand under hand, kicking footholds into the dirt. The hole is deep and disappears in darkness. The grandmothers watch their sons dissipate into shadows until they see only the bald of their heads.

The White
Wings of
Moths

Bea lies in her daughter's bed, in the narrow rut
of the mattress, where the small hips of a stomach-sleeping child
wore grooves between the springs. It is an upper–bunk bed. As
a child, her daughter liked being scrunched tight to the ceiling,
boxed in by pillows, an old drapery-like comforter pinning her
down. Bea is giving this method of sleep a try.

Menopause has made sleep a difficult thing, a hidden room in a
hidden house in a hidden town. She is in her sixth year of symptoms and has come upon a bad time. Her body burns and tingles.
And there's quaking inside her limbs. The bones in her spine have
turned to ice. Her ovaries too. She feels them heavy and cold like
stones nestled against her womb. She knows hormones would

make it all go away but she doesn't dare. Her mother died from a stroke. Bea takes drugs to sleep. They make her hands heavy but awaken her ears. She has tried ear plugs, but the beats and burps of her body make more noise than clocks and cars and dogs. She has tried sleeping like her husband with a pillow between her legs. She has tried sleeping like her son in a perpetual roll that twists and tangles the sheets. She has tried sleeping as her mother did, hands folded over her chest. She tries to occupy sleep from a different body in every bed. Every night, she sweats through every bed in the house. The sheets have taken on a sepia tinge.

All the beds in the house are empty. Her daughter is in Cambodia fixing cleft palate children. Her mother is in a coffin on a pale pillow deep deep underground. Her son is in Pittsburgh with a wife who knits Bea a pom-pom hat every year for Christmas and sends typed recipes for vegan soups. Bea uses the recipe cards to clean the crack between the cutting block and the stove. Since her husband transferred to his new job at the jail in Danamora, she hasn't cooked more than grilled cheese and hard-boiled eggs. Sometimes when she can't sleep, she sits in the breakfast nook with the window behind her open and blowing against her neck. She listens to radio jazz, soaks her feet in a basin of water, and peels hard-boiled eggs. She likes the way her fingernails slide under the shell and sink into the white of the flesh.

Other times, when she's given up on sleep, she walks the streets and collects caterpillars from the trees. At first, she collected them in an old Care Bear thermos. Her daughter did this in grade school, leaving the square sip straw up so they could breathe. A green Good Luck Care Bear is printed on the thermos, though two paws have worn off from the abrasion of thumbs. Now she takes the thermos along for water and drops the caterpillars into a bucket, the handle looped over her elbow like a basket of bread.

She walks the streets between three and five in the morning. She wears shorts and a sports bra. The flab of fat hanging over her caesarian scar would horrify her children, but there is no one around. At first, Bea expected to come across other women with sleepless bodies. She imagined they would congregate in the cold night air and share stories, and this would soothe the electricity under her skin. But out in the night in the dark, she is completely alone.

She takes slow shuffling steps to keep the heat at a simmer. She hits her heels against the pavement trying to shake out the ants crawling between her toes. When she gets too hot, she presses her forehead to the cold metal pole of a stop sign. When the metal warms, she moves on. She goes to the places where caterpillars assemble. To the bark of the Grayson's willow. And the leaves of Mrs. Chin's pear tree. The rose bushes against the library fence. Also the nest in the Okolsky's alder. There, the branches are so thick with bodies that their feces fall like rain.

The caterpillars are plentiful, and it is easy to fill the bucket. When she hears the whistle of the five o'clock train, she goes home and disseminates caterpillars in every room. She started doing this two months ago, when her husband put the house on the market. He's been living in a two-bedroom modular home outside the correctional facility's wall to avoid the two-hour commute. He is a deputy superintendent now. He likes saying these words. Bea sees him two or three weekends a month. He wants her to leave the house and move to the prison with him. He says since Bea's retired, and the kids are gone, two bedrooms are all they need. He uses the word *downsize*, says they should give old toys and clothes to a battered women's shelter. When their place sells, he says Bea will move to Danamora with him. In the meantime, she's supposed to pack things up. She's not in a hurry to empty her life of possessions. And the caterpillars have slowed down the sale.

They've nested in couches and cupboards. They've curled in the fibers of rugs. Her husband took an end table back with him last weekend, and they settled in the space where the table had been. They huddled in a mass with right-angled corners, taking the form of a table themselves. Bea doesn't mind. She likes to tend to them. They are her flock. She fills the wheelbarrow with leaves and drops piles near their dens. She sweeps up ringlets of skin when they molt. She puts cloths under their nests to catch the droppings. It gives a routine to her day since she quit her job.

She's been out of work six months. She was sweating so bad, the patients at the dentist's office complained. Sweat dripped on their cheeks when she cleaned their teeth. She was changing her scrubs five times a day. Her boss told her to take time off. She retired instead. She came home to an empty house.

The caterpillars have filled that space. She watches them string nests in the corners. She thinks about silk streaming out of their lips. She wonders what it feels like to unspool a suspension bridge from your gut. Would it feel like relief? Or would it feel empty? Would she want the silk inside her again?

She studies the nest over her daughter's bunk bed. Silk is strung from the ceiling tiles to the My Buddy doll at Bea's feet. She's in the chill phase now of a sweat. She huddles under the blankets and watches the caterpillars sleep. Their long dark bodies seem like shadows layered in the sinews and folds of their own white walls. When headlights flash on the ceiling and cut through the weave of the webs, the hairs on their exoskeletons glow. Bea wishes she could sleep like that, her hair ablaze, her body levitating like smoke.

Bea hides in her daughter's tree house when the realtor brings clients through. The realtor wears colored tights and has porcelain braces that are supposed to disappear against her teeth. Bea tells her husband that the realtor's hosiery is the reason the house won't sell. Who would trust teal tights, she wants to know. I'd trust tights before I trusted worms, he says. Caterpillars aren't worms, Bea says. They're larva. And in some cultures they're a sign of luck. She hopes he won't ask which.

From the tree house, she can see house lights flick on. The realtor never spends more than two minutes in any room. Right now they're in the kitchen. Bea can see through the window. The wife is obese and standing right near the soft spot of wood by the radiator grate. Bea wonders if they could get sued if the woman falls through the floor. The woman takes a cookie from the table. This morning, Bea let her cream of wheat boil over. The stove is covered with a brown crust, and the house smells like burnt milk. To make up for it, she left snickerdoodles and a note pointing to milk in the fridge. Had she known about the woman's weight, she would have left bran muffins instead. The group hurries fast through the kitchen. The woman takes another cookie, and Bea sinks down on the mattress that serves as the tree house's master bed.

Her daughter retrieved it from the curb and hauled it up with ropes and a pulley. At thirteen, she abandoned her bedroom and slept outside even in winter. The tree house has a roof and two glass windows. Her daughter insulated it by stacking roof tiles under squares of carpet. On the walls, she stapled old coats that the thrift store discarded because they were ragged. They give the impression the place is made of cotton and coming apart at the seams.

At the time, Bea told herself her daughter moved out because she wanted to be high in the air. For that, a tree house was better than a bunk bed. And a streak of independence could be a good thing. But really she knew the tree house's most appealing feature was that it was far away from her.

When Bea spoke, her daughter scrunched her face and rubbed her eyes. From the time she was little, she'd had no patience for anything her mother did and seemed happiest when Bea was in another room. She thought there must be other reasons for her daughter's irritability. She suspected her daughter was teased at school because of her clothes. She liked thrift stores. She liked polyester and suspenders. One year, she shaved her head and wrote chemistry equations on her arms in permanent marker. She wrote editorials for the school paper, questioning her teachers' degrees. Junior year, she stopped eating Bea's cooking and took up a raw food diet. She mostly ate apples and nuts. Two months in, her pants hung off her hips and her skin had a lavender tinge. Bea thought her daughter suffered from being too smart. But she reserved a particular kind of animosity for her mother, and Bea concluded that all these years her daughter had been angry for the very fact of her birth.

She didn't have these problems with her son, her youngest. Until he was ten, he called her Mommy. Then it was Ma. He brought his track team friends by the house for snacks. He asked her to proofread his essays because she'd won a spelling bee in high school. He always said goodnight before he turned in. She didn't have to use kid gloves on him. She didn't have to pay so much attention to the tone of her voice. Bea had never been disliked by anyone before becoming a mother. The dentist at the office where she worked called her "sweetheart." Patients requested her for cleanings because she was gentle. They asked her to stay in the room for root canals and difficult extractions, the kind where teeth needed to be broken apart. Without being asked, she held their hands, and no one ever refused. They squeezed so tight her knuckles buckled together. So tight, it was a relief to hear the tooth let go of the gum. Sometimes when she thinks of her daughter and there's that clench in her chest, she squeezes her own hands. When she lets go, it's hard to uncrumple the bones.

Her daughter sends postcards from Asia once a month now. The latest announced she was losing her hair because there wasn't enough food in the village. She said it was the most alive she'd ever felt. She said people live like this in the world, and it seemed like an accusation. Her daughter signs her postcards with a name that isn't her name. Bea sends care packages with multivitamins, granola, and fluoride but gets no acknowledgment of their receipt. She has strung the postcards across the pitch of the tree house roof like Tibetan flags. A few caterpillars have wrapped around the string. They hang like hoop earrings, and Bea thinks sleep would surely be easier if her spine could bend like that.

She watches a caterpillar lower itself from the roof joists on a long thread. The wind from the window swings it back and forth, a gentle rocking. She gets drowsy watching it sway. She pulls an old quilt to her chin, lays her head on a pillow that's leaking feathers, and closes her eyes. In the tree house, she comes closest to sleep. She thinks it's because of the breeze and maybe the elevation. In that in-between haze between sleep and the sounds of the world, she senses her daughter. She hears her teenage voice cataloguing all the bones in the body, reciting speeches to counter her teachers' lessons. She feels the skin tight on her daughter's ribcage. The gnash of her stomach as it contracts into a fist. Then a tingle as dreams crawl out of the fill of the mattress and burrow into her skin. She knows they're her daughter's dreams. They have her daughter's smell. They smell like walnuts and mothballs and ink.

Her daughter's dreams include fire and masturbation. Tunnels that go down down down. And water that fills all the floors of the school. Once, her hip bones twisted out of place, and she dragged herself down the street with her hands. Once, she misplaced her eyes and the world was dark and she kept hearing guns. Today, her fingers are sharp, and she slices through the skin on her chest. She traces the orb of her breast with her pinkie, slides her hand under the flesh and lifts the whole thing out. She stuffs the wound with grass and goes back for the other. She is careful with the curve of the cut. When both breasts are gone, she wraps her chest in scraps of Mickey Mouse sheets. She buries each organ in its own hole on either side of the cedar. Mosquitos settle on her neck and inject needles into her skin.

Bea lies in the tree house until dark with her daughter's dream in her mouth. She stays until her belly grumbles. Then slips through the trap door and descends the rungs that her husband screwed through the bark. She plants the arch of each foot against the wood before shifting her weight down the tree. She is careful. Her son would take it badly if his mother died falling out of a tree house. People would call her crazy. The caterpillars would die without her wheelbarrow loads of leaves.

Inside, there's a message on the machine from her husband. He won't make it home this weekend. There's a facility golf tournament and they need someone to pull up their score. He says the realtor called. He says Bea should be more careful with the stove. He says he can't believe the worms are back. The exterminator will come again in the morning. Bea should be up by seven to let him in. She should come stay with him for a bit. A few days. A week. A month. Leave the house and let the professionals deal with the bugs. He'll change the sheets on his bed. He'll pick up yogurt and eggs. He's heading to the club for food, but she should call so he knows she got the message. He'll talk to her soon.

Bea retrieves a bowl of hard-boiled eggs from the fridge. They're already unpeeled. Sometimes she builds up a surplus. She sprinkles salt, then takes tiny nibbles, working her way through the rubbery white. She wonders if it'll be the same man this time with the canister of poison on his back that mists through a nozzle. He looked so much like Mr. Rogers from TV that Bea was startled to see him without a cardigan sweater. When he said "neighborhood" twice in a sentence, she asked if he knew the show. He said he did but that his name was Thompson. She hopes he's the one who comes. He was in a hurry and missed the nest in the attic. After he left, she watched a line of caterpillars crawl out from under the fridge.

The first time, he sucked them up through the hose of a contraption meant for bees. He sprayed chemicals around the foundation. He plugged holes and put buckets of water in the basement and gave her his company card. Even with the missed nest, it took a week and extra hours to replace the caterpillars lost. Bea was relieved they'd only had a few prospective buyers in the time between. While the caterpillars were sparse, she guided them to prominent locations—the banister rails, the chandelier, the space between the windows over the kitchen sink. Luckily, no one made an offer. She guesses this time the exterminator will be more thorough. She should supply herself with knowledge. She should think up a plan.

Her son would tell her, Use the internet, Ma. But the computer makes her crazy. The cursor's always disappearing off the side of the screen and she can't get it back without starting the computer again. She'd rather read books. In the attic, she knows, is a box labeled BUGS. She pulls down the attic ladder and climbs up and up and up. The attic is hot, and her face soon drips with sweat. She hunts through boxes. She finds the right one behind a rack of wool suits and fancy dresses. She pops the lid. On top is a book called *Butterflies and Moths*. Her daughter's name is on the cover in permanent marker in five-year-old print. Below it is a book called *Creepy Crawly Caterpillars*. She drags the box to the door and pulls it down the steps.

She comes down sweating. Her hair is wet. Her neck is wet. It's wet between her legs. She grabs a book and heads for the bathroom. She peels off her clothes and climbs into the tub. Her skin is moist against the porcelain. She turns on the tap so water hits her toes. She folds her knees up and scoots toward the faucet until her hair is spread out on the shiny white, all the inches of her back pressed down firm. With coldness pooling around her, she breathes heat out of her lungs. She breathes and breathes and still a furnace rumbles inside her. She worries her heels will melt through the porcelain and water will spill through the floor.

She is thinking these thoughts when something drops into the tub. She lifts her chin and sees a caterpillar flailing above her navel. She inflates her stomach and makes an island for him to beach on. Above her head, a nest is built like a drawbridge from curtain to shower head. Black spots like seeds are caught in the silk. A dozen caterpillars remain behind. Bea scoops up the marooned one and sets him on the floor. Then she cracks open the book, skims through the pictures and reads.

She reads, "Caterpillars have twelve eyes but only see shadows."

She reads, "Caterpillars molt when their exoskeletons tighten."

She reads, "The hickory horned devil caterpillar looks like a miniature Chinese dragon."

She reads, "Birds won't eat banded wooly bear caterpillars because of their hair but skunks roll them over and over until they are bald."

She reads, "Tent caterpillar moths have no mouth parts. They can't eat. They lay their eggs and die."

She reads, "Caterpillars don't have mothers. Before they are born, their mothers are moths."

She closes the book and thinks about the caterpillars that share her home. Caterpillars whose mouths will erase themselves while they sleep. Caterpillar orphans who grow so fat they explode out of their skins. She has to get them out of the house before the man named Thompson comes with the poison. She devises a plan.

Bea is at the end of stage one of operation evacuation. She is plucking caterpillars out of their tents. The silk sticks to her skin. They curl at her touch like hedgehogs. Tuck and roll, she thinks.

This is how her plan works. Caterpillars to bucket. Bucket to empty fish tank. Fish tank covered with cheese cloth on little red wagon at the base of the stairs. Little red wagon with wheels that roll to the tree house where pulleys hoist caterpillars up and up and up. To the safety of the tree. The tree house is their bunker until the poison clears.

She leaves three or four caterpillars in every nest as decoys. She tries to choose ones that look weak. Stage one takes longer than expected. The caterpillars' hair rubs her fingers raw. Her body is slimy with sweat again. When she climbs the stepladder to get the ones near the ceiling, she gets dizzy and has to rest.

It takes until three in the morning to fill the tank. It takes until four to fly them up to the tree house. It takes until five to pack a suitcase and food from the house. She packs a cooler of ice and the box marked BUGS. Then she hoists all of it up. Ten times, she goes up and down the ladder. There is fire inside her arms. Her face is red. The vibration in her chest is loud and fast and bright.

The last time up, she pauses on every rung, resting her forehead against the bark. Her fingertips are numb, her feet alive with the buzz of bees. The wind in her ears makes surfaces spin. Then she's up on the mattress and the door is shut and she's breathing hard. She pushes her limbs away from her body. Her organs bleed together under her ribs. Her tongue is a bloated fish. The mattress sinks under the weight of her steam. Language melts in her head and drips down her throat. And all of it tastes oily and salty and thick.

That night colors come out of the mattress instead of dreams. The color her daughter dyed her hair before leaving for college. The color of bruises on her daughter's legs when she jumped off the garage and landed on pavement. The color ink of the bird she tattooed on her throat. The colors cling to Bea's legs and lap up the salt of her sweat. They feed on her hair and pool into the crevices of her skin. And finally she sleeps. And her sleep is hollow and dark. Her sleep is the color of feces left on the lawn in a bucket the year her daughter moved out of the house and into a tree.

When Bea wakes, the sun has peaked. The exterminator's truck is gone, but a sign in the lawn says EXTERMINATE WITH THE THOMPSON TEAM. There is panic in her chest. Panic about unlocking the door at seven A.M. It is certainly after that. Her head is heavy and syrupy thick. She scrambles awake and trips down the ladder. Three times she misses a rung. She scrapes her knee, and it bleeds.

There's a note on the front door. It says she left the house unlocked, and her husband said go on in and get things done. The house has been fogged, chemicals poured behind the walls. The electricity's flipped off. She should stay out an entire day, then open the doors and windows and wipe eating surfaces with bleach. After that, people and pets can return. Call with concerns.

Bea realizes she's still in shorts and a sports bra on the front steps. She hurries back through the fence and climbs into the tree house. At the top, she's winded. A chill corkscrews down her spine. Her feet are heavy with ice. She huddles under the blankets. Not enough. She pulls down coats from the wall and burrows under the layers, her face peeking out.

A caterpillar crawls up a ski jacket tacked to the wood. The ceiling is a tapestry of white tunnels. The fish tank is empty, except for molted skins, paper versions of living things. The caterpillars have wound silk around the rope attached to the postcards. Cambodia's disappeared under a tangle of gauze. No, the postcards are gone, ingested. Caterpillars dangle from silvery threads. They hang like tinsel. Above them are cumulous clouds with feathers caught in their lungs.

A breeze blows in and the caterpillars sway. Each strand swings in time with the rest. At the height of each arc, the caterpillars curl their bodies up to reverse their course. They lead with their heads. Bea closes her eyes on the circus and slips toward sleep. Everything feels heavy and blurred. All she can do is sleep. Sleep is all there is.

When the sleeping stops, the gossamer clouds have grown. Silk has enveloped the tree. But the caterpillars are gone. Bea's not sure how long she slept. It seems like years. She touches her face to see if her mouth has disappeared. She feels lips and teeth and tongue. She speaks. She says her name. Beatrice. Beatrice. Beatrice. She sings her name, and it lights the layers of silk. She peels back gauze to find the door, slides the bar on the lock and descends.

The lawn glows in the sun. The exterminator's sign is gone. For a moment, she thinks her house is missing too, a circus tent in its place with circus stripes and circus peaks and animals grazing out front. She looks again. The tent is the same shape as her house, and her house is there beneath. Above the chimneys, the tent rises in two points like the ears of a cat. There are pillows out on the lawn, house plants, groceries tied in plastic bags. Signs taped between the stripes read POISON. KEEP OUT. A skull and crossbones, big and black. And other words in tiny type.

Bea follows the front walk and feels through the tarp for the door. She takes the tent in her teeth and bites. It burns her tongue. It doesn't rip. At the corners, the seams are rolled and clipped. The tent is held to the ground with sandbags, red and long like snakes. Bea goes to the back, kicks sandbags out of the way, unsnaps clips as high as she can reach. She pulls the tent apart and crawls beneath. In the bright rubbery glow, she inches her way down the side of the house. She finds the dining room window, presses her fingers to the glass, and pushes up—a broken lock. Her husband opened it once to yell at some kids. The window was locked. He ripped the wood. Bea digs her fingers under the storm window, jiggles the frame, inches it up. A moth with a beard slips out and brushes her neck. She piles sandbags, climbs them like stairs, and hoists herself into the house.

The furniture is gone, but the house is filled with moths, and the moths are filled with light. The light is tinted red and gold and blue, each window hatched with stripes. There's a film in the air like fog. It is furry and coats her throat. She feels movement on her skin. Fans blow the moths from room to room. The space around her is filled with the white of their wings. They brush one another, and the sound of their brushing is soft. In front of her eyes, they flicker and float like pixels on a miswired screen.

Bea slips through the house. She shuffles so she won't crush their tiny paper bones. A smell fills her lungs as she moves. Sharp and sweet, something like fruit with sulfur below. A dentist office smell. She hears the drill. Feels powder on her tongue, the resin used to fill cavities. The air smells like that. She closes her eyes, and moths alight on her skin. Their footsteps prickle. They lift off her arms. They just want to touch her once. They say there is something better upstairs. So she goes.

At the top of the stairs, the hallway is dark. In her bedroom, moths drum against the windows. The dull colored light sends them into a frenzy. They bump other bodies. They bump the glass. The closet doors are propped, and inside, moths pretend to be clothes. Bea touches a dress. The moths flutter apart and reassemble as pants. Bea shuts the closet door and goes back to the hall. The attic ladder is down, and moths usher her to its steps. She climbs, and they follow her up. They steady her legs and guide her hands. In the attic, they are thick like down. They coat the walls. The walls are soft. Around the chimney, they huddle en masse. They smooth the chimney's edges out. They bulge, a tumorous growth, a snowy beast. Bea approaches. She blows them away. Brushes them back. She unearths a cocoon. A cocoon the size of a daughter. A daughter with a bare scalp. A daughter with womanly breasts. And scars on her thighs. A silver pin through her lip.

Quiet Camp

We arrive on a westerly wind, our lungs inflated with speech. Our mothers said this would happen if we didn't learn to quiet our tongues. Our tongues couldn't be stopped, so up we went. Up and up. Until we knocked the chandeliers with our heads and scraped the ceiling with our feet. Our mothers thought we would learn our lesson then and quit our talkety-talk for good. We tried but couldn't stop. We kept talking, and the talking held us aloft. When our mothers got sick of the constant buzzing overhead, they brought us to the docks and launched us into the air. With nothing to bump up against, we rose into the clouds. And soon our mother's skirts were nothing but colorful dots. We cleared rooftops, trees. Now we bob like balloons above a lake. We talk together and all at once. Our talk collides. Our talk congeals. Our talk swells to a roar. What a racket we make. Such noise. Such noise. As we drift to shore and land by a fleet of canoes. Miss Jacqueline waits for us there. She gathers us up, a rabble of raucous girls. Miss Jacqueline says, Hush. Miss Jacqueline says, Shut those clatter traps. Miss Jacqueline says, Little girls should be seen and not heard.

We can talk for weeks without stop. We have special reserves of spit in our glands and calluses on our tongues. Our mouths are caches of fast twitch muscles. A recessive gene, they think, also common in certain frogs and venomous snakes.

A rowdy tribe, we walk through the woods. We carry sticks. We kick at weeds. The sound of our speech swarms like the hiss of cicadas thrashing out of their husks. Syllables tap off our teeth. Our dimples crease and uncrease in a Morse Code frenzy. Blippety-blip-blip-blip. A language of dots and dashes. Of clicks and clacks. Miss Jacqueline says we sound like a meeting of Congolese tribes.

We've seen psychologists and meditation coaches. Speech therapists, etiquette instructors, priests. We've whiled away afternoons in principals' offices, juvenile detention centers, soundproof rooms. We've been punished, bribed, disinherited, shamed, spanked. None of it worked. Now we are here.

We congregate on either side of a long pine table in front of plates of carrots and beans. We can't be quiet long enough to learn each other's names. We can't be quiet long enough to eat. We are always hungry. Our stomachs' whimperings are low hums below the upper registers of our speech. We hold our silverware tight in our fists. Like tuning forks they buzz, and this sound joins the rest.

Noise Machine Chatterbox Loud Mouth Big Mouth Tick Face Busy Body Mosquito Breath Horse Teeth Blabber Mouth Blubber Face Vomit Machine—these are our names.

Miss Jacqueline escorts us to cabins. We climb into bunk beds and pull wool blankets up to our chins. We recite nursery rhymes and jingles to fall asleep. When the wick of the lamp blows out, the darkness exacerbates the noise. We hear howling in the distance, only it sounds like a pack of boys. There's a face in the window, a long-limbed shadow moving beside the door. We recite the Oscar Meyer song for comfort. In the night, our consciousness dislodges, and we slip away. But not the talk. We keep talking, a conversation with no through lines. Non sequiturs spill from our lips, dribble over our chins. Every so often an interjection wakes us up. Miss Muffitt! Her tuffit! Her tuffit! J-E-L-L-O! Hush, Little Tick! In the morning, we feel unhinged.

We pray for recovery. Retreat. Remission. Stillness. We dream. Someday we will hear all of Beethoven's *Moonlight Sonata*. Someday we will hear our hearts keeping time in our chests.

At breakfast, Miss Jacqueline announces the rules of the camp. No speech. No sound. Silence is law. Offenders will be punished. If we think she is joking, we should visit the annex and see the cabinets that house her collection of pickled tongues.

When we were young, our mothers gave us dolls with no mouths. Just a smooth patch of skin under the nose. We fed them bottles through their ears. We learned to administer IVs into their cotton veins. We taught them a system of language spoken through blinks of the eye. When their heads came loose because their blinks were too fierce, we encouraged decapitation. We helped them apart at the neck.

We put on scratchy black swim suits and stand on the beach in the skin of our new silent selves. Language rattles inside us, colliding with organs and ribs. Our hands spasm. Our toes clench pebbles and twigs. Swim test. Swim test. We fight the urge to shout this into the wind. We hold it in, and it wriggles under our scalps. Then Miss Jacqueline blows a whistle, and we step into the lake. Inch by inch, the lake climbs up our legs. And the cold of the water unleashes all of our sounds. We dive into the coldness to stop it from coming. Underwater, words sputter off our lips in a fringe of bubbles. We kick and we kick, trying to empty it out. We surface and gasp for air. We paddle. We stammer. We inhale the lake in gulps. Miss Jacqueline blows her whistle, and we clamber out. Our skin bristles with language. We cough. We wheeze. Sentences froth from our mouths. Twenty demerits each.

We were late talkers. The doctors said developmentally delayed. The first utterance we made was the Eucharist, recited word for word from our cribs. Our first words released a flood. We learned to breathe circularly, so we wouldn't drown. Learning to read was a trial. We couldn't stop talking long enough to hear syllables on the page. Now it is like playing piano. There are two strands of sound going at once. One hand tends to the melody playing above. The other tends to bass notes and chords. We hear them both together. And in separate pockets of our ears.

Demerits mean dish duty. At lunch, no one sits at the long pine table. No one eats carrots and beans. We stand in the dish room with dish rags gagging our mouths. They taste faintly like silverware and bleach. The knots that hold the rags to our necks are hard stones at the base of our skulls. We stand in a line and scrub plates with our fingernails. The dish room clatters as we stack them tall. The dish room bloats with muffled moans.

When we were home, our fathers would retreat to the garage and hide in the caterwaul drone of saws and drills. Our mothers had frequent spells of vertigo and migraines. We are only-children: eldest, middle, and youngest all in one. We once had pets, but they gave us up. We are the sad owners of a runaway flock of hamsters, poodles, and parrots, rabbits, goldfish, and cats.

After lunch, the relay races begin. We crouch on a dirt track with batons and wait for the whistle to blow. It is a silent relay race. If anyone on our team makes a sound, we have to start all over again. So far, no one has made it a full lap. This time, we focus on the old volleyball net at the center of the loop. The net makes us think of fish, and we shout, Mackerel. Cod. Trout. Trout. Trout. The whistle blows, and we jog back to the start. At dusk, Miss Jacqueline gives up the relays, and we run in one long line. We run around and around. The words that hiccup out of our throats match the pace of our steps. Mackerel cod. Mackerel cod. Mackerel cod. We need these sounds in our heads. We fall asleep in the mud with the names of fish on our lips.

We worship the Mona Lisa. Serene and muted in sepia tones. Her lips part wide enough for breath but do not let pass a single word. So she is safe. So she is loved. She is Echo let loose from blurted remarks. And the mermaid relieved of the burden of song. She is Philomena without her tongue. Dun colored feathers sprouting out of her spine. And lit by the glow of the sun.

In the morning, Miss Jacqueline's whistle blows us awake and out of the mud. She marches us back to camp, and we stand in the shadow of pines. A bus rolls through the gate. It seems empty at first. Then a troupe of glowing girls descends. Miss Jacqueline says they are mutes. The mute children parade before us in white frocks adorned with lace. A ring of light hovers over their heads. What ecstasy. What wonder. The lull left behind by flaccid tongues. They stare at our clothes, crusted with clumps of dirt. They point at the sap on our chins, the stains on our knees. As they circle us, we lift our hands to touch the gauze of their lips. We open our mouths, and questions emerge. Where do your voices go? How do you clear your throats? Does silence feel like silk?

At school, the boys only asked quiet girls to the spring cotillion. We noisy girls went by ourselves. We danced in a crowd, singing along. When a slow song came, we danced with each other, the syllables of our words keeping triple time with each waltz. We stood so close, we could feel one another's breath on our cheeks. We put our heads together and whispered into each other's ears. We liked the way this duet filled the space in our minds. It didn't last. Before the song ended, the nuns yanked us apart.

When the mutes are gone, Miss Jacqueline leads us into the woods. We are supposed to listen to nature as we walk. We are supposed to take the scent of pine into our lungs. But those mute girls are in our heads. The thought of them rips through our throats, and we shout out fragments of hymns. Miss Jacqueline keeps track of our demerits as we hike. The path is steep. The forest is thick. We find a pair of boy's underwear on a cushion of moss. Miss Jacqueline pretends not to see. We hike until the moon cuts through the trees. Then we stop and we sit and Miss Jacqueline takes us away from the group one by one. She makes us identify the noisiest girl in the camp. Everyone names someone different. She ties us each to a tree. From our posts, we cannot see anyone else. She leaves us there, with bark scraping the skin off our wrists. We shout into the dark, blaming the one who turned us in. When the owls hoot, we vibrate the cords in our throats until we find the same pitch. Then a whistling noise shoots over our heads, and the owl falls from the tree. We scream and we scream.

We want to be quiet, but we are allergic to silence. Silence raises hives on our skin, induces vomiting, seizures, cold sores. When we stop speaking, our heads fill with a storm of patter that dents our cranial walls. We talk to empty our bodies, to dispose of the grime that cruds our lungs.

In the morning, our throats are raw, and it's time for arts and crafts. Miss Jacqueline passes out rope, and we weave thick braids and tie them together with knots. When we are done, we each have a cradle of rope from which to suspend a potted plant. But then Miss Jacqueline fits them over our heads and pulls them tight. They hold our lips together like muzzles so all we can do is whimper. We do camp chores like this. We wash laundry, collect firewood, sweep the cabins, make our beds. It takes until dinner to bite through the rope. As we do, we release a string of the shrillest yelps ever unleashed from our lips. Demerits all around.

Our parents tried to muffle the noise by padding our rooms with foam. Our voices soaked through the foam and bled into the walls. They rattled through the crawl space and charged the fiberglass insulation with an electric hum. The frames of our houses came alive with a terrible thunder. The light fixtures trembled. Our voices reverberated in windows, mirrors, and the strings of our grandmothers' harps.

Because we ate through our muzzles. Because we did not listen to nature. Because we are obstinate girls who cannot keep our sounds to ourselves, we are sent to the stocks. We learned about the stocks in school. At Colonial World, we tried them out, but our heads slid right back through. Miss Jacqueline's stocks are tight and bolt shut with a lock. They are scattered at intervals on an old cow path covered in clover. The path winds through the woods. In the first hour, our arms fall asleep. In the second, our knees lock up. Hour number three: our necks are sore with splinters, and our backs are cricked. Then it is dark in the woods again. To pass the time, we call each other cunts. We are passing the time like this when a boy comes through. He carries a string of dead rabbits and a rifle. He stops and listens to our chants. One by one, he reaches under our skirts. He searches until he finds a hole. When we scream, he knows he's in. By the time the boy gets home, he is deaf, and pee has dripped down our legs and into our shoes.

For our mothers' birthdays, we always make life-size cutouts of ourselves. We prop them in our chairs at the dining room table. We position forks in their cardboard hands and napkins on their laps. Then we hide in the attic until the day is done. This is the best present we could ever give. One day out of the entire year when our mothers can have daughters that are perfectly silent, perfectly still.

When Miss Jacqueline comes down the path, we are talking like loons. The Muffin Man, you know. Hey diddle diddlely do, the cat peed in my shoe. Miss Jacqueline pulls a needle and thread from her bag. She is adept at looping the thread through the needle's eye. She kneels on a cushion of moss, squeezes our lips, pushes the needle through our skin. Her stitches are small. Her knots are tight. The needle's prick is sharp. The pull of thread displaces blood but it feels like relief. We touch the black thread with our tongues. When we try to say words, the sounds are thick and round and tumble down our throats. We try to say thank you, but it sounds like a snicker. Miss Jacqueline lets us out of the stocks, and we unfold our spines. We march back to camp and drink pureed carrots through a straw and crawl into our bunk beds to sleep.

Mother, may I jump? Mother, may I sing? Mother, may I tip my head in prayer that I might become a quiet girl someday? Mother, may I have a sip of tea? Mother, may I wear a pretty dress? Mother, may I curtsy to the man at the door? Mother, may I move? Or listen? Or breathe?

It is the day of the big canoe trip. We paddle out to the middle of the lake and break for lunch. We drink carrot juice through straws. Then we paddle some more. We paddle until blisters form on our palms. Until Miss Jacqueline's Camp becomes a row of teeth on the shore. When stars poke through the sky, Miss Jacqueline plucks our paddles away and heads back in her own canoe. We try to follow. We try to paddle along with our hands. Our laps get wet, and puddles pool around our feet. The water crawls up our skirts and over our knees. We hum to ourselves until we fall asleep. In the night, our canoes drift apart. When we wake in the dark and look around, we see nothing but lake. We sway with the rock and lean of our boats. We try to call to each other, but the stitches hold tight in our lips. We inhale deep breaths through our nostrils and focus it at the back of our throats. A high pitched hum flits over the lake with the taut legs of water bugs. The sound finds the opposite shore and echoes back. We hum a gentle tune. It is the lullaby each of our mothers dreamt and sang to us in the womb.

Beanstalk

————— ▬▬▬▬▬▬ —————

Lucy's baby is born green, face splotched with yellow like variegated leaves, hair wispy white, corncob silk. All across his body, tiny buds are sleeping. On his arms, a dusting of moss. Veins spider from his chin to his temples and ears. Only his feet are the color of flesh, but not in that pink baby-soft way, more sallow like roots. A philodendron baby. A baby verdant and lush with chlorophyll stirring inside his skin.

After hours of labor, Lucy sees him only a moment while a nurse suctions his mouth and nose. She reaches out and touches his cheek, cool and glossy, the texture of wax. Philip stands by the bed, bewildered. The word *green* whispers its way around the room. Eyebrows rise and fall. Foreheads furrow. Then the baby is taken for tests.

A nurse stays behind to tend to Lucy. She presses her stomach, kneading it back to its pre-pregnancy shape. "Is he okay?" Lucy asks. "Why did they take him away?"

"They're just running some checks," she says.

Philip hovers, a skittish squirrel, watching the nurse's movements. Sweat lifts from his forehead like condensation and trickles down his chin. "According to Gallup's Health and Healthcare Poll," he says, "birth defects occur in one in thirty-three babies, around 3 percent per year."

"He's not defective," Lucy says.

"Of course not," the nurse answers. "He wanted to be a green baby. So that's what he is."

"What does that mean?" Philip asks.

The nurse touches Lucy's knee. "Sit tight," she says. "The doctor will be in to confer." Then she disappears into the hall.

"I didn't mean he was defective," Philip says. "I meant defects are rare. I meant he's probably fine."

Lucy doesn't answer. She turns on her side and strokes her swollen stomach. Philip paces, his loafers stretched so wide the stitching has popped along the sides. His monogrammed shirt has come untucked. His glasses are askew on his nose. He keeps his eyes on the floor until he sees the doctor's shoes.

Doctor Peters comes in with a clipboard. "What do you know?" he says. "A green baby. That's a first. We get blue babies all the time. Dime a dozen, those. Of course, they clear up once they get some air. But your guy is sticking with this green business. Stubborn. Must get that from his pops." He gives Philip a robust slap on the shoulder. Philip jumps.

"He doesn't need oxygen, then," Lucy says.

"Nah, his breathing's fine. Vitals stable. Nothing serious."

"Except he's green," Philip reminds him.

"Oh, yes," the doctor says. "He certainly is that. Best we can tell it's some kind of algae. Probably from your water pipes. You drink water?"

Lucy nods.

"Well, there you go. Keep tap water away from the baby. No

breast-feeding. You've probably got algae still in your system. Get bottled water. Feed the baby formula. We'll give you some sample packs."

"It's okay that he's green?" Philip asks.

"We can't say it's okay," the doctor says. "We really don't know. The green should go away on its own, but we can't be sure. Either way, tomorrow you can take him home."

"That's it?" Lucy says.

"I'll send in a nurse for a crash course in newborn care. The staff will help through the night. Doctor Briggs will check the baby tomorrow. If he's good, you can go." He gives Philip a vigorous handshake, winks at Lucy, and disappears into the hall.

Then the nurse is back with the baby. She places him on the bare skin of Lucy's chest. "It helps with the bonding," she says. "Babies like to feel skin."

The baby wraps his fingers around Lucy's silvery hair. He yawns, and his tongue, small and green like a lizard's, darts out of his mouth. He smells wild and sweet like rain-soaked soil. His silky white hair coils into delicate springs. On his forehead, a bud has started to swell. He smiles at his mother. He is beautiful, she thinks, like no one has ever thought to be beautiful before. And even if it means he's defective, Lucy is glad he's green.

The nurse sweeps a tendril away from the baby's face. "Let's not hide those beautiful buds," she says. "They'll need light to open." She adjusts the sheet, and her braid swings over her shoulder. Lucy tries to remember when her hair was dark like that. In adolescence, her hair grayed strand by strand, so now at forty-six, she seems decades older, hair silvery-white, frame shrunken to bones. Skin hangs from her arms like valance curtains. The flesh around her eyes sinks in like forgotten fruit. Lucy's reflection reminds her of fairy-tale witches, lips pulled down to their breasts, breasts pulled down to their knees, noses crooked at peculiar angles to better smell children lost in the woods.

"Let's see if he's hungry," the nurse says. She pulls a baby bottle out of her pocket. "We'll start him with water to check his digestion." She turns the baby so his head is in the crook of Lucy's arm and hands her the bottle. "See if he'll take it. Just hold it up to his mouth."

A few drops fall on his lips. His tongue darts out, and he latches onto the nipple.

"That's quick," the nurse says. "It usually takes newborns a while to figure it out. He's hungry. That's it. Tip up the end, so he doesn't get air."

Philip leans over Lucy's shoulder. She can smell the tuna sandwich he ate at noon when her contractions were still twenty minutes apart, and all she could do for the pain was squat on her hands and knees on her living room carpet, her back arched like a cat. Meanwhile, her senile mother and Philip munched their tuna and eyed Lucy with curious glances as though she was a piece of performance art.

Now Philip presses against her shoulder and rubs the mossy fuzz on the baby's arm. His touch is light and cautious, as though the baby were likely to bite. "I've heard that 42 percent of infants lose the hair they're born with," he says, "in two or three months."

Philip is a Gallup Poll Caller, the only paid-by-the-hour employee she knows whose job brings him absolute bliss. He logs the most polls in the state, calculates standard deviations on napkins, and shares the results with postal workers, bus drivers, cashiers, and Lucy, of course. It has always intrigued her. But now she suspects she is an emblematic figure to him: a mid-range American woman, middle-aged, middle-class, averagely attractive, somewhat smart, sometimes happy, often depressed. Who would want to be that?

The nurse catches a dribble of water on the baby's chin. "You're right," she tells Philip. "Sometimes their hair grows back a different color. Some infants look entirely different by the end of their first year."

"More normal?" Philip asks.

"I'm glad he's green," Lucy says.

"Of course," the nurse says. "He's a beautiful baby."

"He has my features. A little Philip Jebediah Junior."

"Is that his name?" the nurse asks.

"We're still deciding," Lucy says. The baby looks nothing like Philip, and she's grateful for that.

The nurse tips the bottle higher. "You can take your time

with the name. You and your husband can even wait and decide at home."

"He's not my husband," Lucy answers.

"Oh, I'm sorry."

"I'm the father," Philip explains.

"We're neighbors," Lucy says.

She's known Philip almost a decade, since the day he followed her home from the park and sat on the stoop of her building, reciting a poll about pets. He talked until the sun went down and Lucy got cold and invited him in for a sandwich and tea. At midnight, he was still talking, quoting polls on the Pope, male pattern baldness, and mumps. She sat and listened, fascinated by this strange person who'd come into her home. She could see he was hapless and gentle, a bearer of little-known facts. At least, he'd be good at Trivial Pursuit, she thought. Salt and pepper hair wisped out of his nostrils. He chewed his sandwich loudly, condiments spilling onto his chin. But of all the people in the park that day, he'd picked her, as though he were some kind of scout. And she had thought that meant she was wholly distinct.

After their first meeting, he came by often with grocery-store pie. They talked and talked, and their conversations were lovely secrets that made her feel smart again. When the apartment across the hall opened, he moved in. Thousands of conversations later, after hundreds of pies, countless rounds of Trivial Pursuit, three ice storms, two leap years, and one episode of sex, they'd ended up here.

Lucy hadn't meant for the sex to happen. That day, she'd woken up on the couch, the television murmuring static, the living room dark as though clouds had buried the sun. But the sky was bright beyond the window. A curtain of leaves was blocking it out. Overnight a vine had grown up the building, tentacle fingers digging into the brick. Lucy slid open the window and touched the bristle of roots that had clawed through the rusted squares of the screen. The leaves on the vine shivered under her finger, and a tremor ran through her scalp. She put her cheek to the screen and peered up the building. The vine reached up to the roof and arced out at the eaves, stretching into the air as though it intended to use the sky as a foothold all the way up. Lucy had an inkling to climb it, to dig her toes into the stalk and inch herself into the clouds. She imagined geese circling around her, their lungs filling up with noise.

She still had her face to the screen when Philip knocked. With the feeling of flight caught in her hair and a checkered pattern pressed into her cheek, she closed her eyes and kissed him. They stumbled to the couch, where he unbuckled his belt, and she slipped out of her skirt. She held a finger to her lips. "Shh. Mother's sleeping."

Their bodies slid together. Hips jerked and heaved. His glasses fell to the floor. Then her mother coughed in the bedroom. Lucy froze, and a shudder ran down Philip's back.

Her mother shouted, "Lucy, I need you." So she crawled out from under Philip and scrambled into her clothes.

In the days after, she avoided him. Then the nausea started and the tenderness in her breasts.

"You didn't use a condom?" her sister Fay had scolded.

"I'm menopausal," Lucy said. "I haven't had my period in months."

After Philip heard she was pregnant, he came by multiple times a day. Before, she hadn't minded his visits. But the more the baby grew, the more Philip annoyed her. She couldn't listen to more statistics. She couldn't eat another piece of floury pie. When he knocked, she shut the lights and feigned sleep.

She hadn't wanted him there for the delivery, but Fay said he was, after all, the father, so Lucy relented and called him when her contractions hit. She let him drive her to the hospital and hold her hand through the birth. But she made sure everyone knew they weren't married. She put a big X next to *single* on the insurance papers and when she introduced him to the doctor and nurses, she enunciated the word *friend* clearly. She said it slow. But this nurse here had missed it. Lucy wants her to take it back.

"He's not my husband," she says again.

"I'm sorry," the nurse says. "I just assumed when I saw the ring."

Philip holds up his hand. A gold band stamped with a G squeezes the flesh under his knuckle. "I work for Gallup. I got it for superlative polling," he says.

Lucy is quiet. The G on his ring *is* for Gallup, but it wasn't earned. He bought it on his fortieth birthday. The men at work wore wedding bands, and since Philip felt he was devoted to Gallup in a similar way, he let his co-workers think he was married. Outside work, he told a different story, said the ring was a token of Gallup's appreciation for his allegiance to their team. He's explained it so often, Lucy imagines it now is truth in his head.

A silence falls over the room. For a long moment, no one speaks or moves or breathes. Then the baby hiccups, and everyone looks.

"Wow," the nurse says. "Done already. He was thirsty."

"Can I hold him?" Philip asks.

"Sure," the nurse says. "But let's have you take off your shirt. We'll put him right on your chest."

Philip blushes. "That's okay. I'm fine with it on."

"No, really, it'll make him feel safe."

"Maybe later."

"Oh, come on," the nurse prods. "Mama here's been naked all day. The least Papa can do is bare his chest."

He fumbles with his buttons, the red in his face traveling down his neck. Lucy wills the buttons to cling tight in their holes. She doesn't want him to hold her baby. She snuggles him under her chin. A bud on his forehead splits into a six-petaled flower. When she touches the blossom, his hair flutters. A smile spreads over his lips.

"Hello, my little baby," she says. "Hello, my little Jack."

"Little who?" Philip asks.

"Jack," she repeats, and the baby smiles again.

"What about Philip Jebediah Junior?" he asks, his shirt unbuttoned, belly exposed.

"He doesn't look like a Philip," Lucy says. "He has the look of a Jack."

In the morning, Lucy wakes in the hospital to the sound of rustling leaves, her breasts heavy, pelvis aching. She feels a tickle on her neck, the flesh of a flower brushing her ear. "Good morning, my baby," she says, and cups the flower in her palm. Another one opens on the vine that's crawled up the bed.

She swings her legs to the floor and looks over the plastic

aquarium walls of the crib. A tangle of vines grows out of the silky mane of his hair. He smiles up at his mother and kicks his blanket. She gathers the vines and tucks them into his sleeper. A few leaves come off in her fingers, tiny leaves with points like a crown. She slips them into her pocket and lifts him up. His mossy arms are soft against her shoulder. His hair flutters with a crinkling sound. "Shh," she whispers and turns her back to Philip, still asleep in the reclining chair across from the bed, his feet jutting out so that all night long, when a nurse came with a bottle, the door bumped his feet. Now, his arms hang to the floor, and he snores, chin slumped against his chest.

In Lucy's arms, the baby squirms. His hair twists and arches, reaching toward the water pitcher beside the bed. Lucy dips her fingers into the pitcher and drips water into his mouth. All through the night at feedings, he turned away from formula bottles. She knew he wanted water, but the night nurses wanted to get nutrients into his blood. After hours of fighting, Jack's body slackened. His arms and legs went limp. Finally, exhausted, he took the formula bottle and emptied it quick. An hour later he was awake and writhing, a sticky sap oozing out of his pores. Lucy wet her pillowcase and wiped him clean, then filled his bottle with water and fed him until he closed his eyes.

The rest of the night, he slept soundly. The stir of his hair lulled her to sleep. She is used to nights in her apartment punctuated by her mother's labored breaths from the bedroom, cries for help to get to the toilet, insults muttered at a husband two decades dead. For once, Lucy's sister has had to care for their mother. And although the nurses woke Lucy every three hours to feed the baby, she still got the best night of rest she's had in over a year, since her mother's eyes went foggy and she fell down the stairs and came to Lucy's apartment to live. For the first time in months, Lucy unclenched her jaw in her sleep. For the first time in months, she dreamed.

She dreamed she was pregnant in high school, walking the halls in a pleated skirt with vines growing out from between her legs. The vines grabbed at teachers, wound around books, bore through lockers, and split the linoleum floor. The students stood against the wall and held mirrors. Lucy watched her reflection appear and disappear in the circles of glass. She saw high school

Lucy. Lucy before masturbation. Lucy before W-2s. Lucy who hadn't written a eulogy yet for her father or touched her mother's naked skin.

Back then, she had been thin like a bird with hollow cheekbones and knobby knuckles. Her nose was bent at an obtuse angle. Her breasts were concave things. She had shriveled peach pit elbows and knees, eyelids purple from skimping on sleep. She stayed up late memorizing the dates of battles, chemistry tables, Latin conjugations, the number of flats and sharps in the major scales. She hated this information, the way it marched back and forth in her head in heavy boots and wool uniforms with thick fringe hanging off its shoulders. Sometimes the armies collided, C sharp mixing with Robert E. Lee, parabolas falling into physics equations, Macbeth's tomorrow and tomorrow and tomorrow speech creeping into metatarsals and the geography of Soviet states.

When graduation came, she refused college. No more information. Her head was tired. Her parents were elated. Their other daughter was sixteen and pregnant. Lucy could join the workforce and help with the bills. She got a secretarial certificate, then a job at a realty office, where she typed leases and eviction notices, took rent checks, and answered the phone.

At first it was nice, the mindless typing. But after awhile, she wanted something else. She tried community college, but she'd forgotten most of her science and math. She couldn't memorize formulas and facts as she had in high school. The endurance to push through thick novels was gone. She quit college before her first semester ended and went back to the realty office. With school behind her, she tried not to think of all those A's—though they were the last thing of merit she'd done.

But now she's grown an evergreen baby, and she feels like the world has changed. She goes to the window to see. When she parts the curtains, the buds on Jack's forehead stretch open. A tendril of hair wraps around her thumb.

By late afternoon, the bags are packed and Lucy waits with them at the curb. The baby has been checked and named: Jack Philip Knolls-Dalton, the birth certificate signed twice. The nurse with the braid, back for the day shift, holds the baby in his car seat as Lucy climbs out of the wheelchair, and Philip pulls up the car. Lucy opens the back door, and the nurse sets the car seat in. When Jack's buckled up, the nurse touches his forehead. "Sweet little baby," she says. "Just like a little shamrock. This one will bring you luck."

Lucy checks to see that the car seat is wedged in tight. The nurse smiles and hands her a stack of formula packs. "From the doctor," she says, "though I doubt you'll need them. Any fool can tell he's not that kind of baby." Lucy sets the formula on the floor mat. As she turns, the nurse presses a baggie of little brown pellets into her hand. "Miracle Grow," she says. "From me. The hospital wouldn't approve."

Lucy slips the bag in her pocket. Her eyes catch the nurse's name tag, dangling from her neck. "Rose?" she says and smiles. "Thank you." She shakes her hand.

"You take care," the nurse says, and kisses Lucy's cheek.

Lucy climbs into the car, and Rose shuts the door behind her.

"All ready?" Philip asks.

Lucy nods, and they head for home. In the mirror, Lucy sees Rose wave as they pull away. Her braid whips in the wind.

Philip is quiet. He drives slowly, braking before every bump.

"I'm sorry about the name," Lucy says.

"I always wanted a son named Philip Junior."

"If it had been a girl, I wouldn't have called her Lucy."

"I don't see what's wrong with my name."

Lucy turns to check on the baby. His car seat faces backward, so she can only see the top of his head. The setting sun filters through the trees and ripples over his hair. She reaches back and strokes the silky strands. A vine shoots out and catches her wrist. She tries to untangle herself, but her body's twisted. She releases her seatbelt and turns around on her knees. "Are you crazy?" Philip shouts. "Do you know how many passengers fly through windshields a year?"

She unloops the vine from her wrist and slides back around. "His hair was caught on my hand," she says. "I'm fine."

Philip stops at a yellow light. Lucy watches it turn red. They stop at every light for fifteen blocks. "Philip, the last two were green," she says.

"I'm just being careful. A car going the other way could run a red."

"Okay. I'm sorry. I'm just tired." She leans against the headrest and shuts her eyes. She feels leaves climb over her shoulder and tickle her neck. She smiles. A rustling fills her ears. She is almost asleep when the car jerks to a stop. Her seatbelt tightens. "What's wrong?" she asks.

"I can't see out the window."

Jack's vines have spread into the front, leaves pressed to the glass. Lucy laughs.

"It isn't funny," he says. "I could have hit something. A kid on a bike. Or a puppy."

She pulls back the leaves. "No puppy," she says.

"I can't drive like that. It's not safe."

Lucy sighs. "I'll sit in back." She gets out of the car and goes around. Jack smiles when he sees his mother. "My little beanstalk," she says, and gathers the vines. She wraps them around her hand like a wreath and sets the bundle on her lap. As the car starts forward, she strokes the leaves between her fingers. They crawl over her thighs and enfold her hands.

At home, a sign hangs from Lucy's apartment window: WELCOME, BABY! The letters are outlined in marker, filled with blue highlighted over in yellow, a makeshift green.

Lucy unbuckles Jack's harness and slips the wreath of leaves through the hole. She tucks them into his blanket and folds the corners in to protect his feet from the early evening cold. Before she can climb out with the baby, her sister Fay runs down the steps. Her sheer-pink blouse matches her lipstick. Her high heels make a clip-clop sound. She takes the baby from Lucy. "Let's see my little nephew," she says. "Oh, how precious. Just like a little frog."

On the way to the hospital, Lucy called Fay to pick up their mother, so she wouldn't be alone all night. In the apartment, their mother usually watches talk shows while Lucy's at work. When Lucy gets home, her mother tells her the talk show stories. Fay brings a casserole once a week, and Philip comes with pie.

When they leave, Lucy bathes and powders her mother, makes her tea, and tucks her into the apartment's only bed. These last few months, her mother has taken to saying, "Ah, what a time to be pregnant. At your age, you'd be better off with a dog."

Lucy had hoped Fay would take their mother away for the week, leaving her apartment quiet and empty. Instead, Fay is here, and Lucy can bet, her mother is just where she left her in the rocking chair with a cup of cold tea on her lap.

Fay is two years younger than Lucy. She had her son in high school, her daughter two years after that. Her husband George got a job at his father's paper supply company. Fay stayed home. When her kids got to high school, she dedicated herself to the Mary Kay Corporation, easing the anxieties of middle-aged women with foundation, mascara, and blush. She says she'd help more with their mother, but she's got her hands full with the business and two fully-grown derelict kids. Lucy hopes she'll be a better mother than her sister. She worries as Fay slings Jack over her shoulder, one arm under his bottom, the other gesturing up at the sign. Lucy stands close as they head up the walk. She sees the panicked look in her baby's eyes. Then a vine shoots out of his blanket and loops around Fay's hoop earring. Fay feels the tug.

"Trouble already," she says. "Just like my Jimmy."

Lucy unravels the vine, tucks it into the blanket, and kisses his head.

"How you feeling, sweetie?" her sister asks. "How's the vagina? Doesn't it hurt like hell? I can't imagine it now at your age. God bless. You must be exhausted. We brought food."

"You and ma?" Lucy asks.

"And a few welcome-home guests."

Upstairs, Fay's husband George and her son Jim have taken over the love seat and are watching football, hands buried in bags of Tostitos and plastic containers of dip. Sure enough, Lucy's mother sits in the chair where Lucy left her, wearing the same clothes. She's asleep, mouth open wide. The mug of tea on her lap has been replaced by a sign that says CONGRATULATIONS and a bowl of mixed nuts.

On the couch, a row of ladies sit together in loud blouses and heavy makeup, their hair sprayed into unnatural curls. Deviled eggs and bruschetta lie on silver trays before them, next to a pot of tulips with plastic stems. The ladies hold gift bags lined with green tissue paper. They smile wide at Lucy. She's never seen them before, though she can tell they're Mary Kay ladies, ever ready to play gal pal to a forty-six-year-old new mother whose sister says doesn't have friends of her own.

Fay scoots Lucy to an armchair and hands the baby to a lady with a shiny gold blouse. She turns down the TV volume, says, "Jim, say hello to your aunt."

Jim turns toward Lucy, gives a casual wave and stares at Jack.

"He's gorgeous," the Mary Kay lady says, beaming.

"Yes," says another. "Just like a little elf."

Philip stands in the doorway until the conversation pauses. Then he walks into the room embarrassed, like a student late to class. He sits on the floor by Lucy and crosses his legs. She can picture him sitting this way in grade school, his legs too round to tuck his feet in. She feels a wave of affection for Philip and rests her knees against his back.

"I remember when Sheila was this little," the gold-blouse lady says. "She's in Wyoming now with her boyfriend. He's Buddhist. Sometimes I wish she was a sweet little baby still."

"I know," a woman in leopard-print says. "They're never this innocent again."

"And you just look great," a woman in polka dots tells Lucy. "I'll tell you, after I had Daniel, I was a balloon. My doctor scolded me for getting fat, but I got even fatter when I had Tina. Bill divorced me when I hit two-hundred pounds. But you look fantastic. Look at those thighs. And your stomach has just shrunken back in."

"You'll be a terrific mother," says the gold-blouse lady. She passes the baby to the next lady in line. "You have that nurturing look."

"Thanks," Lucy says. She stares at the pot of plastic tulips. Fay's always been good about center pieces and hors d'oeuvres.

"What's his name?" the leopard-print lady asks, stroking the baby's cheek.

"Jack Philip Knolls-Dalton," Philip announces. "The Philip part is for me."

"Ah, yes, I can see he resembles his father."

"He has my features," Philip says.

A commercial comes on, and Jim grabs a beer from the fridge.

He stops at the couch and stares at the baby. "He doesn't look like Philip," Jim announces. "He looks like a fern."

Fay slaps at the air. "Oh Jim," she says.

The leopard-print lady passes the baby along. In the passing, his blanket slips open, and all the vines spill out.

"Oh my," the woman says. She tries to tuck the branches in, but they unravel onto the table. The gold-blouse lady grabs the bruschetta. Another picks leaves off her lap. A vine wraps around the pot of tulips and drags it to the edge of the table. Fay's hand flies out and snaps the stem. Jack's hair rustles in furious spasms. His limbs curl into his body. Lucy grabs her son.

"I'm sorry," Fay says. "It was instinct." She rubs his back.

"Get out of my house," Lucy says.

The leopard-print lady sweeps the clipped vine under the couch with her foot. Another collects the deviled eggs. Jim grabs his case of beer from the fridge. George takes the chips. Fay strokes Jack's head. "He'll be okay, Luc. Really. Babies bounce back. I'll stop by at the end of the week?"

Philip shuts the door behind them. He paces the kitchen. "I'll call the doctor."

"No," Lucy says. "He just needs purified water. Go to the store." Philip looks around the apartment with frantic eyes. "Get a system on a stand," Lucy says, "the office cooler kind with the plastic jug on top." He nods and goes.

With Philip gone, Lucy takes the bag of Miracle Grow pellets out of her pocket. She dissolves them in a bottle of water and feeds the baby. When half the bottle is gone, the shaking stops. Lucy walks back and forth with Jack nuzzled against her breast. A vine wraps around her arm and cups her elbow. He lets the bottle drop and closes his eyes, and she sets him into the crib.

"So you had a baby," her mother says, startling Lucy. "I didn't think you would."

"His name is Jack," Lucy says.

"And he isn't retarded?"

"He's perfect."

"Babies are never perfect."

"This one is."

Lucy helps her mother to the bathroom, holding her under the armpits while her mother pushes a walker and shuffles. As she walks, her mother farts. "Oh dear," she says. She's soiled her pants. In the bathroom, Lucy lowers her mother onto the toilet and peels off her clothes. Her underpants are caked and dirty. Her shoes are wet.

"I didn't think you were coming back," she says. "I thought you went to another country."

"What country did you think I went to?" Lucy asks.

"You were always talking about Nepal. I thought you went there."

"Didn't Fay tell you I was at the hospital having the baby?"

"She did, but she didn't want me to take a bath, and she couldn't find my nightgown."

"Didn't you tell her your gown was under your pillow?"

"I didn't know," her mother says.

Lucy runs the water until it turns hot, then helps her mother into the tub. She gives her a washcloth and soap and sits on the toilet, watching her mother dab at her breasts. Bubbles float up in the water. "Oh dear," she keeps saying. When she's done, Lucy washes her back and rinses her hair. She pulls her up by the armpits, her mother's heels squeaking against the tub. Lucy towels her hair dry, slips her gown over her head, and tucks her into bed.

Then she checks on the baby. Jack is asleep, a soft sound whispering through his hair. Vines have escaped from his sleeper and spill out through the wooden slats of the crib. Lucy sinks down on the couch. Her body aches. Her breasts are heavy. A milky liquid leaks onto her shirt. She pats at the wet spot with the edge of the afghan, then pulls it around her and closes her eyes. When Philip returns, she's almost asleep. He drags in a water dispensing system on a dolly. It clunks over the lip of the doorway. "Is he okay?" he asks.

She nods. "He's sleeping."

He looks into the crib. The armpits of his shirt are damp. His face is red.

"He's fine. Really," she says. "Show me what you got."

In the kitchen, Philip rips open the box and gets to work setting the water dispenser up.

"It's nice," Lucy says, and kisses him on the cheek. While Philip is busy, she gathers her mother's clothes in the bathroom and sets them in a bucket to soak. When she comes back, Philip has finished. His shirt is wet. He lingers in the doorway, stretches his arms, and yawns. "Long day," he says. "I think I'll head to bed. We can sleep at my place."

"The crib's here," Lucy says.

Philip nods. He turns the knob and heads across the hall. When he's gone, she feels a sudden panic. But then he's back, wearing flannel pajamas, carrying his toothbrush, a pillow, and a glow-in-the-dark Gallup Poll clock. He drags the coffee table to the side, tosses cushions off the couch and yanks at the metal handle until the pullout bed unfolds with a snap. The mattress is creased into thirds under crumpled sheets. He throws the afghan over the covers and fluffs his pillow. When he lumbers onto the mattress, the wire frame creaks. He lies on his back, his hands on his chest. Lucy stacks the cushions against the TV console and picks Tostito crumbs out of the rug.

"The water stains on your ceiling look like Abraham Lincoln," Philip says.

"I never noticed." She goes to the kitchen and drops the chips in the sink.

"Come see."

He pats the bed, and she sits on the edge. She leans back to view the brown mark on the ceiling. His shoulder is warm against her cheek, and she rests her head there. His pajamas are soft. When Mrs. King in apartment 12C takes a bath, the ceiling drips. Lucy tries to find Lincoln in the sepia stain. But to her, the shape looks like a monkey. She doesn't tell him this.

"According to a February 2007 Gallup Poll," he says, "Americans consider Lincoln the greatest U.S. president ever, though in 2005 Ronald Reagan beat him out."

"I voted for Carter," Lucy says, and nestles into his neck.

"According to a 2001 President's Day Poll, 76 percent of Americans know that Lincoln's wife was Mary Todd."

Lucy lifts her head. She can see where he's going. She sits up. "You chilly?" she asks. "I've got more blankets in the closet."

"A recent Gallup Poll found that 91 percent of American adults have either been married or plan to get married in the future."

Philip loosens the ring on his finger. He yanks it over his knuckle and holds it out on his palm. The G is upside down.

"Philip, I can't."

"You didn't even let me ask."

"I'm sorry," she says.

Philip squeezes the ring back on his hand. He opens his mouth, but nothing comes out.

"I'm sorry," she says again.

Philip pulls the afghan over his stomach and turns on his side, and Lucy slips away.

In the bathroom, she locks the door behind her and turns the knob in the tub to hot. She strips off her clothes and studies herself in the full-length mirror on the back of the door. She looks old and tired. Her arms are boney, her stomach swollen and sagging like elephant skin. She looks nothing like a new mother. She touches the bags under her eyes, then hangs a towel over the glass to block her reflection out.

She climbs into the shower and pulls the water release. Hot water streams over her head. She leans into the tiles. Water has never felt so good. She slides to the floor of the tub and crouches on her hands and knees, letting the water pummel her back. Her head drops between her shoulders. Her body crumples. She puts her cheek to the porcelain surface and weeps.

When Lucy comes back from the shower, Philip is snoring. He lies on his back, his limbs sprawling over the mattress. She checks on the baby. The buds on his forehead have closed for the night. She strokes his glossy cheek, then crawls onto the foldout couch. Philip's body is turned to the wall. Despite the shower, her feet are cold, and she tucks them under his leg. She nuzzles into his back and puts her arm over his waist. But she can't find a place for her other arm. She tries it behind her, then over her head. Philip turns on his stomach, and Lucy rolls onto her back. She folds her legs into a pretzel to warm her feet and listens to the rhythm of his snores until she falls asleep.

In the night, the same dream replays again in her head. She's in high school walking the halls, vines growing out from between her legs. She gathers them in her arms. The bundle of branches gets bigger and bigger and still the vines come. The halls are empty. She's late for class. Her feet move quick. She's running. The hall gets longer and longer. Then she's in a bathroom with hundreds of stalls. She ducks into a stall painted green, squats on the floor, and pulls up her skirt. The vines unthread from somewhere deep inside. The leaves are white and printed with numbers. She plucks them off and piles them in a stack. She tries to study the numbers, but they don't make sense. She yanks at the vines, pulls faster and faster. They rip her skin, and she feels the wetness of blood. Still the vines get longer. Enough notes. No more. Where is the baby? She pulls and pulls. Nothing comes but leaves. Leaves covered in numbers. Numbers she's never seen. Then the bathroom door crashes into the stall, and she jolts awake.

She tries to sit up, but there's something heavy over her chest. Philip's arm. The room is humid and hot, and she can barely breathe. She tries to shift. The metal bar under the mattress digs into her ribcage. She's pinned. She wiggles her arms out of his grip. Her nightgown's wet. Her breasts are leaking. She smells like sour milk. From outside, a streetlight shines on the crib. The crib looks empty. She listens. Nothing. She holds her breath and focuses her eyes through the dark. No baby. She scrambles out from under Philip and crosses the room.

The mattress is covered with leaves. She pats them with her hands, and they fall through the slats. "Jack?" she whispers. "My little bunny, where are you?" She lifts up the edge of the mattress and runs her hand along the wood. She gets on her knees and feels on the floor. Her fingers collect lint from the rug, leaves, but nothing else.

Philip stirs. "What's wrong?"

"Nothing," she says. "Go back to sleep."

"I'll help," he says, fumbling around in the blankets. "Is he okay?"

"He's fine. I just dropped a diaper." She pats the floor, crawling along the baseboards, her pulse beating inside her head. Where could he be? She perks her ears, listens for the rustle of leaves. There's a crinkle under her hand. A trail weaves its way to the kitchen. She follows. The edge of the carpet is wet. A curtain of vines grows over the doorway. She steps through. In the kitchen, water pools around her feet.

"Jack? Baby? Make a sound so Mommy can hear you." She slides her feet over the floor. Her foot clangs against a teapot.

Red microwave numbers shine in the dark. The water dispenser's empty. Vines climb the walls and wind through cupboard handles. Leaves cling to the curtains. The fridge is buried in moss. Jack lies in a puddle, branches growing out of his body, roots clawing into the floor. She puts her hands under him and tries to lift. But he's anchored down. She kneels in the water and touches his head. His hair weaves through the tines of her fingers and sets off that rustling sound.

Then the bed creaks, and Lucy hears footsteps. She lies on the floor and wraps her arms around her son.

"Lucy?" Philip says. He is just beyond the doorway. She can see the top of his face through the branches.

She buries her face in the peaty sponge of Jack's belly, closes her eyes and lets the scent of forest rush into her lungs. Flowers crawl over her body. A lattice of vines surrounds her. Water soaks into her skin.

Landscapes
in White

1

The sky full of feathers, a quarrel of wings. Plumage blooms across our windows, the glass smeared cloudy with milky streaks. The beltway a blur of sparrows. City towers beaten by doves. The ponds in the park untidy with chickadee bodies, breasts buoyant, claws branching up without leaves. A gull bursts his larynx murdering sound. Squawks rend the August heat. Wings beaten bare. The sky thrashed white. Sudden squall of quills and petals. The ones thick with mites fall fast and pierce the ground like arrows. The downy ones linger. You stand on the sidewalk and catch them on your tongue.

2

Roofs unhinge and houses unpage in the wind. A flurry of phone book listings. Newsprint ripped and torn by trees. Fall's foliage stamped with Garamond font. Moths bridled to paper wings. The Book of Ruth stays aloft on exhalations. Shredded tax forms drift like milkweed seeds. I prop the aluminum ladder against the house and unclog the gutter. I piece the scraps together and read the words aloud. You pluck paper out of the sky and fill your pockets. You bury the scraps across the yard and water the little mounds. A coupon lands on your shoulder. A receipt sticks in your hair.

3

February early dark. Iridescent rain unthreads the sky. Raindrops gorged on nitric acid streak the sable skin of night. The streets are air-raid empty, people bottled in glass. Rain's pounding lodged in our brain space. Comets scratched on our eyes. The furniture smells of sulfur. Carpets mildew underfoot. We wear masks to bed to block the light. We lie on plastic sheets. You slip out from under my arm and go to the window. In the glass, you swim through fire. Stars sew seams through your skin.

4

When the rain stops, the world is missing its flesh. We walk on its bones—bleached rock and stratified plastic that flakes underfoot and lifts in the breeze. Grit in the air. A gauzy fog. You part the webs with your fingers. Filaments catch in the hair on your arms. Up the road, a crew in florescent orange steamrolls the crumbling ridges. A truck pours asphalt over the plastic. A man in a visor rakes the asphalt smooth. The air smells of burnt hair and tar. You hiccup, and a petal of plastic slips into your lungs.

5

The skyline is burning. Towers drip and melt like candles. The sky scallops with smoke. Windows burst. We spread blankets and watch the explosions. They fracture the night and split the air with sound. The children squeal and cartwheel in the street. Their palms turn white with ash and make marks on their clothes, handprints left by ghosts. You wave a sparkler around like you're conducting the disaster. It catches without a match.

So Much Rain

Butternut says if houses wore dresses, ours would have to lift up its skirt so rain wouldn't soak into its ruffles. Cupcake says if our house's joists were legs, the water would be past her knees. Puddleduck says by tomorrow the waves will splash up on our house's panties. Butternut says, Your simile stinks; before giving a house panties, you have to liken her base floor to a lady's snatch.

Tonight's dinner is tulip wallpaper peeled off the master bedroom walls. We prepare it in a saucepan over a Yankee candle fire. When the candle gets melty, we drip wax over the tulips. That flavors them nice. The candle's got a Holly Berry scent. Mmm, Mmm,

Puddleduck says. Tastes like Mama's earlobes. Cupcake says, Better enjoy these delicacies while you can. Sonny's bedroom has sailboats on the walls. Butternut says, Please pass the yellow tulip with the mottled chartreuse stem.

Puddleduck wakes up from her nap in a fret because water's soaked into her bum. Water's soaked into all our bums. Best move our nap upstairs. Too bad. We liked taking naps in front of the fireplace. Even though there was no fire. Only ash. Now ash floats on top of the water. We pretend the ash is krill and open our mouths wide like whales. Rows of baleen line our jaws and filter the part that is fish from the part that is sea.

We try to remember Mama's name. Butternut thinks it was Carol. Cupcake thinks it was La'Shawn Juanita O'Shea. Puddleduck thinks it was Benadryl. No, Butternut says. Benadryl was the name of your cough syrup. No, Puddleduck says. My cough syrup's name was Luanne. Then she folds her knees into her nipply boobies and squeezes her teeth tight to remember how Luanne tasted on her tongue. She remembers how Luanne burnt her throat and made her tonsils ring.

Butternut made up a game. Here's how it goes. Everyone closes their eyes and counts to a hundred. But Butternut only uses numbers made of glass. Cupcake only uses numbers made of ink. And Puddleduck only uses numbers made of snow. After we say all the numbers, we open our eyes and see which have managed to float. So far Butternut's won the most games but only because she made up the rules herself.

The master bedroom has been mined dry of tulips, so we rip down some sailboats for lunch. Sailboat sandwich. White sailboats on top and bottom. Green and red sailboats between the bread. Condiments: wallpaper glue, aged to yellow flakes, slightly sour, a hint of salt. Like horseradish, Puddleduck says. No, mayonnaise. No, paprika pickle spread.

It's too wet in the house now to sleep. Our hair is wet. Our toenails are wet. Our pee holes are wet. We haven't slept in two days.

Cupcake says all the sleep's leaked out of the house. Butternut says we should sing a song to make it leak back in. What song? Puddleduck asks. The one about the peacock, Butternut says. How does that one go? It starts do-wee, do-wee.

Puddleduck calls the others to the bathroom window. She thought she saw a serpent sliding over the water. It had rainbow hair and eyes like fiery globes. Was it wearing a top hat and britches? Butternut asks. The one I saw yesterday looked like that. Serpents don't wear clothes, Puddleduck says. Cupcake laughs, and Puddleduck swats her sister. Shut up, she says. That serpent could carry us straight to Mama's new home.

We try to sleep in the room with sailboats formerly on its walls. But the house is sloshing back and forth on wobbly legs. Cupcake gets the idea to string our sleeping bags up like hammocks. The mattresses are gone, so we tie our sleeping bags to the bunk bed frame, one on bottom, two on top. In our hammocks, we feel like caterpillars wrapped in cocoons. We pretend we are growing wings. Still we're wet. Still we don't sleep.

Tonight we eat Polaroid squares from the family album. Not our family. The Wilcox family, who previously owned our house. Our family's all here except Mama. Mama set off to sea to find us a spot of land with fruit trees and a goat. She set off in an orange paddle boat, propelled by her feet. We sent her away with blankets so she wouldn't get cold in the wind. How many days ago did Mama leave? Butternut says twenty. Cupcake says eighty-four. Puddleduck says two thousand and three.

Five days and no sleep. Purple rings around our eyes. We call each other names. Raccoon breath. Corpse face. Battered wife. Puddleduck is delirious and says silly things. She says, Toothpick pirates kicked my thump. She says, Olive oil axed the kittens. And— Global warming ate Mama's syrupy eggs. The eggs that were supposed to be our brothers? asks Cupcake. Puddleduck shakes her head no, then yes, then no.

Butternut found crayons stuck in a crack at the back of the closet. One stick blue. One stick pink. We take turns coloring each other's teeth. Cupcake's top teeth are all blue, her bottom pink. Boys on top, girls on bottom, she says. Butternut wants hers done every other tooth. Puddleduck's favorite color is pink, so she sticks with that. We bare our teeth at each other and growl our ghastly grins. And all night while we're awake and not sleeping, our tongues steal tastes of wax.

Cupcake says, Last night I dreamed Mama got swallowed up by a whale. How'd you fall asleep? Butternut asks. It was an awake dream, Cupcake says. It was the same whale as Jonah's, and Jonah was still inside. You got it wrong, Butternut says. Jonah got out of that whale. Well, he must have got back in, Cupcake says. Now let me finish the story. Mama jumped Jonah's bones inside the whale. And they both had little whale babies, two a piece, whale baby twins. And that's where all our brothers have gone, Puddleduck says. No, Cupcake says. Our mama don't bear boys. The whale babies were all baby girls.

The water's halfway up the wall where the sailboats used to be. It's washed out the bottom hammock, so Butternut's bunking with Cupcake, and Puddleduck's all alone. She lets her leg flop over the side of her hammock. Her toes taste the salty waves. Next to her, Butternut and Cupcake tangle their limbs around each other so they won't knock each other out of bed. Puddleduck listens to their cooing noises as they nestle into each other's skin. She hears them whisper. Cupcake says, Do it like the brothers. Do it like this. The salt on Puddleduck's toes makes her shiver. She misses Mama's kisses on her nose.

Mold is eating our nightgowns. Butternut makes a declaration: no more clothes. Not even bathing suits? Puddleduck asks. You want a soggy crotch? Cupcake says. Puddleduck shakes her head no. They drop their gowns out the window and watch them swim away, jelly fish with lacy wings. Then they splash around on the stairs leading up to the attic. They climb to the top and leap into the hallway below. The water slaps their skin and it feels like a spanking. They run to the stairs and do it again.

We only have enough Polaroids left for one more meal. One a piece. Cupcake nibbles at a picture of three brothers holding a giant Hershey bar on their laps. She eats the heads of the brothers last. Butternut eats a picture of a man and woman holding hands in front of a train. Puddleduck eats a picture of a Mama with a baby on her lap.

Butternut has a new game. It involves holding our breath. We dive under the water and swim down to the first floor and bring up whatever we can find in our teeth. Today, Cupcake brought up a latch hook rug. Puddleduck brought up a water gun. Butternut brought up garden gloves. You dope, says Butternut. Plastic is inorganic. You can't eat that. Cupcake and Butternut curl up in their hammock and share their snacks. Puddleduck fills the gun with water and aims it at their heads.

We had to abandon our hammocks. The water swallowed them up. At night we lie at the top of the attic stairs. Tell me a story, Puddleduck says. Which story? The one where Moses's Mama splits open the ocean so Moses can gather pearls for his sister? No. Not that one. The one where Jesus's Mama teaches him to do pirouettes on top of the water to impress his brothers? Uh uh. The one where Noah's Mama sings a lullaby over and over so the dove can find the Ark? Yeah, that one, Puddleduck says. I don't remember how it goes, Butternut says. And anyhow, it was an ostrich, not a dove.

While Butternut and Cupcake scout out the attic, Puddleduck watches the window. With her head on the top step, the horizon stays in view. She keeps watch for the serpent or Mama or Jonah's whale. The house rocks back and forth on the waves, then lurches and falls and hits with a slosh. Uh oh, Puddleduck says, sounds like she's fallen off her legs. Good thing the fat lady floats. Then a wave comes through the window, carrying seaweed and plastic pellets and a lump of feathers and fur that finds a home in Puddleduck's lap. She thinks it is a tiny brother's head. And that means Mama must be close.

The attic has one tiny window and rafters and splintery walls. Boxes are stacked to the ceiling. Butternut and Cupcake rip them open. They are filled with seashells padded with foam. The girls tear at the filling and binge 'till their bellies are full and shards of shells circle them like the bones of a meaty meal. They lie on pieces of cardboard and stare at the light from the tiny window. When the house falls off its legs, Butternut says, Uh oh. Sounds like she's gone off the deep end. Yeah, Cupcake says, She's giving up the goat.

When Butternut and Cupcake come down with heavy bellies, they see that Puddleduck has found a pet. It's a dove. No, an ostrich. No, Sleep's washed back into the house. Can we hold it? Be gentle, Puddleduck says. Butternut and Cupcake take Sleep up to the attic and sit on a piece of cardboard with their new pet between them. They run their fingers through its fur. They pick seaweed from its feathers. Butternut tells it a story in French. Sleep climbs up her hip, then her ribs, and cuddles into her collarbone. Then they all shut their eyes and sleep and dream of buttermilk beaches typeset with footprints missing their toes.

When Butternut wakes up, Cupcake is rocking Sleep back and forth in her arms. She is telling it a story about a brother who raped a bird. She says, This is how he does it. Fly away to the land of the goat when he's done. Butternut interrupts the story. Where's Puddleduck? she asks. She went to the kitchen. Into the water? Where else? Cupcake says. That's all there is. She go for food? No, Cupcake says. She heard Mama calling downstairs.

In the kitchen in the space under the cupboard under the sink, Puddleduck can hear Mama sing. Mama sings the lullaby that brought the ostrich to Noah's ark, the ostrich with a fortune cookie in its beak. At the end of the song, Puddleduck is out of air. Time to kick to the top. She waves good-bye to the water. Goodnight, my little Puddleduck, Mama says. Sleep well. She rolls a bottle across the kitchen floor and leaves it at her feet. Puddleduck hugs it to her chest and kicks. One floor. Two floor. Three floors up.

Our fingers and toes are icky like prunes. They've sopped up so much water, they look like pickled grapes. Each hand bends into thousands of creases. We sit in a circle and read each other's palms. Sleep perches on Cupcake's head. Butternut's palm says she will marry the king of Equatorial Guinea and give birth to Alaska. Cupcake's palm says she will invent a uterus big enough to envelop the entire sea. Puddleduck's palm is hard to read. Too many dangling modifiers, Butternut says. And a mess of incongruent verbs.

The water's up to our knees. We fill the bottle with water and pour it out the window, but the water level doesn't drop. Pretty soon it will lap against our thighs. It will lick our vulvas clean. What's the bottle for if not to drain the water? It's for our sins, Cupcake says. What will we write them on? Butternut says. We ate the paper and crayons. Just whisper them into the bottle, Cupcake says. The glass will remember. Glass is good like that. They whisper, Bless us, Mama, for we have eaten the Wilcox family and stolen their house. We waterboarded the beach. And overconsumed the well. We couldn't birth any brothers. And we murdered Jonah's whale. But if you come again to judge the waterlogged sisters, we will wish away the rain.

We pile all the boxes up and climb on top. The water's made them wobbly, so we sit close and hold each other for balance in the dark. Cupcake's boobies are getting big. They poke Puddleduck's knee. Puddleduck shifts her weight and kisses Butternut's cheek. Sleep hops from head to head, and when she gets hungry slides down Cupcake's shoulder and nurses at her breast.

Tomorrow we'll go up on the roof if we can fit through the window. If not, we'll call the obstetrician. Or start a synchronized swimming team. Or stir ourselves into starfish soup. While there's still air, we take turns holding Sleep above the water. We take turns telling stories. And singing the lullaby that will make the ostrich come.

Six Sisters

6

When the morning sickness subsides, I crave canned peaches, slippery fat on my tongue. Pits cored out of their bellies. Bodies embalmed in juice. The skin so supple my teeth sink all the way through, hewing the fruit again and again. Nothing sharp to pierce the palate or scrape the throat. So the bits slide down leaving a sticky sweet film. So the mass of it settles in the sling of my stomach. So my lips meet the edge of the can and my head tilts back and I swallow the fluid in hungry gulps.

I drink so fast I miss the thing floating deep in the syrup. A tiny fetal girl disguised as just another scrap of peachy pulp. I swallow her with the rest. And only realize that a girl is falling down the deep dark hole of my throat when I feel the syrup swirl over her head. The syrup catches on her peach fuzz hair, and I know it's Estelle. Estelle who grew as big as a cherry, then let go of the womb. That was a year ago. Maybe two. She let go and slid into an airplane toilet. I was on my way to Phoenix to visit my parents after my father's stroke. On the phone, my mother said he spoke now with a lisp and couldn't balance fruit cocktail on his spoon. I stayed with them for a month. I called Carl once a week. I had never told him about Estelle. And she knew.

Estelle knew lots of things. She knew how the thought of taking care of people made me sweat. She knew I only stayed with Carl because my house had shitty pipes, which he had the patience to unclog, and I didn't. She knew that I douched with bleach after the pregnancy test turned pink. She knew that before my father's stroke, I hadn't spoken with my parents in over a month. And still another week went by before my mother told me the news. She waited until he left the hospital and was home in his bed. Why should you worry? she said. We're managing fine. When I hung up the phone, my underpants were spotted with blood. I changed my clothes. I booked a flight. I chose a seat over the wings in case the plane came apart in the air. I read an article once about a crash. Two survived. The wings protected them in the fall. But on the trip to Phoenix, the wings didn't make a difference for Estelle. She fell into the toilet, that tiny metal bowl. I flushed fast, and the suction changed the smell of the air. It felt like losing a tooth, like a gaping hole in the gum. The plane trembled, and I worried the wings would let go. Then the wheels slammed down, and only relief was left.

Now she's come back. She somersaults through my intestines and then is still. She rests, and I say, Little girl, why are you here? Did you come because there's a baby growing inside me again? Did you come to see if I would want a boy more than a girl? Carl says it might not be a boy. It's only week six, too early to tell. But the vomit that rises in my throat each morning smells male. Like raw onion sweat and that yeasty semen smell. The smell fills me up. It spreads to my fingers and toes. I can taste it in the skin I bite from under my nails. That smell finds Estelle through the tiniest of pores. And I say, Don't you wish you had stayed in that can, burrowed deep in a den of fruit? Syrup is sweeter than blood and so much softer than love.

5

Week eight. Cold feet. Cold despite the thickness of August air, the tautness of heat suspending saliva and mud. It's never heartburn. Never tender breasts. But every time. Week eight. Cold feet. Carl sleeps in the guest room now with the window unit on. He's left me the big bed and flannel sheets and windows wide, breeze pressing in like warm breath. This morning, he brings a cup of tea and a printout of the cell counts in our mice from all of July. Homework, he says. He's heading out to mow the lawn. Lab goggles are strung around his neck, old leather dress shoes on his feet. He fears a pebble will careen off the mower and gouge his eye. He doesn't own sneakers or loafers or boots.

The tea has steeped too long and is like rancid almonds on my tongue. I pour it into the aloe plant on the sill and huddle under the covers, turn the TV to an old episode of *M*A*S*H*. This is me pregnant in August. Wrapped in flannel. Wool socks pulled up to my knees. They are old socks. My mother's socks. Darned with yarn that doesn't match. A clever hiding spot for a girl. Hidden at the tip of the toe, braided into the weave. She is just a few cells held together by blood, but she crawls from the fuzz, following the path of a thread. She slips under the nail of my toe. The skin splits and she's in. And it hurts as much as if she'd splintered the bone. Then she digs her way up, traveling close to the skin. Over the ankle. Straight up the femur. She rests under the cap of the knee. Little Bernadette. Who left so quickly in the night. I had only been working with Carl a month in the lab. She was his, and she left so she wouldn't get his cleft in her chin or his squarish face or hair the color of lead. She knew these things would make me cringe. So this time she comes in rough and makes her entrance hurt. Because I told Carl children were parasitic things. Like barnacles. Like lice. Like fleas.

4

I tell Carl I'm done with work for awhile. Bed rest. To make sure this one takes. Doctor's orders? he asks. No, I say. I don't want to take any risks. Moving around in the world is a dangerous thing. So I'll be slicing mice brains alone? he asks. Afraid so, I say. Think of me and the mice while you sleep, he says. I will, I say. But I don't.

I spend all of week eleven in bed. While the mice sink into a lobotomized haze, I huddle under the sheets. I sleep and I sleep. She finds me there. Hester. Hawthorne's slut. A chip off the old block. An apple falling close to the tree. She hatches from an egg buried deep in the mattress, rips her way out, and scales my chin. She shimmies up my nose hair with marsupial grace, slips into the nasal cavity, and rappels down my throat. Mountain climbing girl. Artist of the trapeze. Mama's little babe, her first concern was always to please.

She left so I wouldn't get fat. That summer I was the thinnest I'd ever been in my life. My muscles ached. I could do fifty push-ups and a seven-minute mile. When I jogged, men in cars turned their heads to follow my stride. I ran until my vision blurred, then went to bed without a snack. I slept with eight different men that summer, two from the lab, six from the gym. Only one I remember well. On Thursdays, I did the climbing wall. Hester's father held my line. He wore Tivas and said, You win the prize, when I tapped the top. The harness cut into my crotch. I climbed until my fingers were raw so I'd be the last one left before they closed and could ask him to drive me home. I was scared of heights. Hester is not.

Like a bat, she hangs upside down in my tracheal tube, listening to air currents whistle in and out of my lungs. I tell her to pay attention to the voices, the songs swirling around in my blood. Hester, my girl, the one I can trust, What did Estelle and Bernadette say to the boy to make him loosen the bolts on my bones, leaving my pelvis unhinged? Did they say I have formaldehyde breath? That I boil eggs for lunch and dig out the yolks with my thumb? That there's a five o'clock shadow in the pits of my arms? The smell of death between my teeth? Dear Hester, swallow these sounds before they are sucked through the cord and into the meat of his fists. So he won't hate me too.

3

The house reeks of mothballs. The walls feel close. The boy is flitting around. He moves like a moth. The frantic motion quickens my pulse. Sweat pools around my neck. That smell eats into my lungs. The chemical tang of it hurts my throat. But no mothballs are to be found.

I wash everything. Sheets. Blankets. Coats. I string telephone wire from tree to tree and hang everything out in the yard. The coats droop and graze in the breeze. I sit in the grass and watch for their tongues. I wear only a robe. My thighs press into the dirt, molding themselves to the leaves.

I don't notice the bite until the next morning. Until I am naked. Counting varicose veins on my legs. Bull's-eye scar. Horned insect burrowing in. Burrowing. Burrowing. Always the way at first before the claustrophobia sets in. I get the tweezers and pinch the head of the bug. But the girl breaks loose and wiggles away. I dig and I dig. But she's gone.

Carl slept at the lab last night. Some of the mice are dead. And you, little girl. Eunice, right? From graduate school. From the boy in the chemistry lab with ink on his lip. You would have had Asian eyes and tiny thumbs. But you slipped down a shower stall in the locker room at the pool. And the boy in the lab. Before graduation, he published a statistical proof that included a P value, a Y, and an X.

2

They call me into work to check the results. I get out of bed. In the lab, Carl shows me the mice who are still alive. When he leaves for lunch, I let out the ones who show remorse. The rest I put to sleep. The results are inconclusive. No patterns. Nothing learned. I go home and write letters to the girls graffiti-marking my womb. I explain how the lobes are arranged in the skull. The circuits crossed and recrossed and braided into intricate lace like the red and blue lines on my breasts. I tell them about my father, who worked at a canning plant, who has freckles on his eyelids and broke a rib on a sled as a kid. And my mother who was only ever a mother, who soaks fruit in rum on Christmas Eve and wears paperclips on her bras when the clasps fall apart.

Then I tell them about me. How the fruit in my fridge molds before I can eat it. How it seems to mold faster than other people's fruit. How I scrubbed off the enamel that made my bathtub shiny. How I scrubbed my teeth so hard I eroded the gums. Not the kind of person you'd want teaching you how to eat and sleep and breathe. Little boy, I'll try harder if you stay. And if you could please stop flailing around, that would be a great help as well. The hard little pit of your hard little self is slamming into my ribs. Stay still for an hour or so, and I'll leave the bathwater cool so your skin doesn't boil red. Then we'll get that sandwich meat you like.

November is the month of baths. I fill the tub and reread the letters I wrote to the girls. They seem just right, and I drop each page into the water as I am done. They float above my belly, a belly rounder than the one I wore last week. And the ink from the letters drifts away from the pulp. Then the water seems moldy too. So I use my mouth as a net and swallow all the tiny inky legs. Deep in my stomach, the lines of the letters tangle and twist and turn into a girl. Little Yvette. Daughter of a drama club boy. But you weren't the artsy type. You stayed up nights with me studying calculus. You held on to the formulas I couldn't fit in my head. My little math genius. You would have been scholarship material. An Ivy League girl. But you fled. In a hot tub over spring break, you started to trickle out. My roommate teased, made Lou Gehrig jokes. She thought it was my period. I'd been pregnant a month and had read all the books. I knew what it was, but I didn't tell. I swam into the ocean, farther than all the surfboards and rafts. Until the people on the beach were a forest of tiny trees. I shimmied out of my bikini bottom, held the fabric in my fist, and floated on my back. Yvette trickled down my leg and filled up on salt and sand. I wondered why she left and what it meant. If it had something to do with the one who took up residence first. When I got back to shore, my cheeks were burned from the sun.

Now Yvette drops fistfuls of sand as she paddles through a current of alphabet soup. She kicks through the debris until she finds the other girls. She shows them the fragments of letters I wrote. In pieces, they don't make sense, but they sound like a poem. The girls read the fragments over and over. They recite them to the boy. So he won't go out of his mind. Trapped for twenty weeks with only his thoughts. His head knocking around in a terrible fit. In a sandbag made of skin.

1

It is December and there is snow. Snow in the crevices of crispy leaves. On the blossoms of auburn mums. I kick my slippers onto the walk and let the frosty blades of grass slip between my toes. I have always loved to play with ice, its slow insensate ache. I tilt back my head, and snow sprinkles my face with tiny delicate bites. In this ash gray haze, I find my first tiny girl. She falls from the clouds. A sliver of ice that pricks the lobe of my eye. She melts her way in, slipping over tissue and organs and bones, like a raindrop in search of a drain. Farther and farther in. Until she finds a pillow and rests her head. It took her the longest to find her way back. Because of the way she left. The other girls creep close and stroke her hair while she sleeps. Her parts are inside out, making her prettier than the rest.

Eliza Rose. You came to me on a bus. Way way in back. With the smartest boy in the sophomore class. He got a perfect score on his PSAT. I wanted that to be me. We would meet in the chemistry lab during lunch. We burned things. I loved the smell of chemicals on fire. Sometimes I would masturbate with a glass vial and he would watch. His name was Lee. I knew that the glass could break inside me, but I did it still. It made Lee forget how to speak.

We had sex under a pile of coats on the bus. On a field trip to Colonial Williamsburg. Where the women wore wool underpants, wool stockings, wool corsets, wool skirts. In a field filled with sheep and snow, I bled and I bled. It had been my first time. But you were already in. And the things that you thought and the things that you were scared me out of my mind. I brought the glass vial home from school. I hoped it would break. And it did.

Eliza Rose, you curled around a shard and nuzzled into its blade. Now you've found your way back. You sleep with your head on my spleen. You think nothing and nowhere and of no one at all.

When you wake from your nap, they will tell you about the boy. His restless squirming. His flailing limbs. How he hammers his fists into my bladder until it dents. How he bends back my ribs and scratches words on the wall. They have tried talking to him. They have tried singing. They are out of tricks. It's your turn, they will say. Eliza Rose, tell him where you've been. And you will explain what happens to children whose mothers let them go.

Dye Job

On the bus to school, Lily sucks fat purple grapes through her lips. Ruth tells herself to stop staring, but her eyes lock tight on Lily's mouth. She watches until Lily catches her watching, then hops across the aisle and squishes into Lily's seat. Lily clutches the bag of grapes to her chest, snarls, "Do you have to sit so close?"

"Did he invite you yet?" Ruth asks.

"Stop asking," Lily says.

"Are you sure you're eating enough?"

"If I eat more grapes, I'll barf."

Lily's eaten nothing but grapes for a month. *Chic* magazine says grapes boost natural pheromones, attracting the boy of any girl's dreams. Lily's got her eyes on Bobby Litchfield, a senior with biceps thick like tree trunks and dimples on his knees. He's Lily's number-one hottie, and she's laid her claim for prom. But as a ninth-grader, she needs him to do the asking. So she's taking *Chic's* advice to heart. Now, it seems there might be a catch.

Ruth holds Lily's arm up to the bus window. "I think you're turning purple," she says. Lily's skin has always been pale like marble. Now, after a month of Concord grapes, it's marble with a lavender tinge.

"It'll be hot," Lily says. "I'll match my prom gown."

"You sure this is safe?"

Lily shrugs. "Like I care."

If Lily's health remains unaltered, Ruth will embark on the all-grape diet too. She wants to go to prom with Lily's brother Felix, who has green hair like truffula trees. Felix is the only nineteen-year-old junior at Crow Hill Academy. He repeated fifth and sixth grades. Lily tells everyone her brother's disabled, says he can barely read. He's done summer school six years in a row to get ahead for basketball season so he can keep steady C's and stay on the team. Ruth doesn't care. She's seen him read cereal boxes. That's enough for her. Being a good reader is a worthless talent. Felix can launch balls so they whoosh through the hoop like exhalations. He can run endless loops around their cul-de-sac, his lungs filtering infinite air. And he's got a particular talent for yelling at Lily so her chin trembles, and her voice splits apart. Ruth wants to be good at things like that.

She's in awe of the way Felix and Lily argue. They live next door, and Ruth sits on her porch roof, peering through windows as the madness climaxes in violent shrieks. No one at Ruth's house ever erupts like that. If Ruth screamed at her sister, her parents would make her walk to oboe lessons for a month. But Felix and Lily are never punished. Their mother, a psychiatrist, works late and is often away at conferences, leaving them free run of the house.

When their mother's gone, they throw parties. Lily's supposed to stay at Ruth's house. She isn't allowed alone overnight since her mother caught her in bed with Drew Krause. Not that it matters.

When Ruth's parents turn in, Lily slips out the bathroom window and climbs down the tree at the edge of the porch's roof. She's back before the party peaks, tucked under the covers on Ruth's hideaway bed, so when Ruth's mom cracks the door and asks if they can sleep through the noise, Lily squints in the light from the hallway, and in her groggiest voice says, "What's going on? Is it time to wake up?"

The kids at school tell Ruth, "She's using you. She treats you like garbage." But Ruth thinks, "Not as much as I'm using her." She peers into Lily's room from the bathroom window, watches her dance to Avril Lavigne, hair swinging loose, hands levitating overhead. She watches her practice pouty looks in the mirror and strut in odd amalgamations of clothes. It's how Ruth learned to walk down the hall at school with a saunter in her step. Even if Lily ditches her most of the night, Ruth is glad she comes over so she can watch her sleep and floss and eat Cheerios one by one off a spoon. She watches the way Lily skips down the driveway, only the tips of her toes touching gravel. She watches her climb on the bus without touching the rail. And in the eighteen minutes it takes to get from their cul-de-sac to school, Ruth keeps track of the tiniest details. Like now, the way Lily checks her hair in the window. And now, as the bus takes its last turn, how she wiggles her skirt, exposing a sliver of skin. And as the bus pulls to the curb, and the first bell rings, how she lingers on that very last grape, her tongue tasting the deep dark purple before her lips spread wide to take it in.

At lunch, Lily crowns herself the first ninth-grader of the year to bag a prom date. She shows off her phone with Bobby Litchfield's text. The girls lean over their blue lunch trays, the only color the popular clique selects from the stack. "How'd you do it?" they ask.

Ruth busies herself unwrapping a hummus sandwich so she won't blurt the secret out.

"It's the purple thing, isn't it?" Claire asks.

"It's totally hot," Brittany says. "Is it glitter?"

Lily shakes her head no.

"You have to dish."

Ruth sits up higher. Lily made her vow to keep quiet. But now Lily's got the date, Ruth can't resist. "It's the grapes," she says.

Lily scowls. The girls live next to each other but aren't the kind of best-friend close that makes it okay to spoil stories. They are close in proximity, have been this sort of close since Ruth's mom started driving Lily to preschool after her parents' divorce. But they never had much in common. And now, as ninth graders, they have less in common still.

"Ruth's a moron," Lily says. "Thinks she's so smart. But I'm the one with the prom date. I'm the one who knows." She pinches a grape between her fingers. "It's not just any grapes. They're Norman Concord. And you have to suck the juice like this."

"What's so special about Norman?" Ashley asks.

"It's not the brand," Ruth says. "It's probably the polyphenols in the skin."

"Well, you go eat your poly-whatevers and we'll eat Norman. Trust me, girls. It takes three or four weeks, and then, you look like this."

"Like flamingos," Ruth says. "Flamingos turn pink from eating shrimp."

"Who cares about flamingos?" Lily says.

Claire slides a napkin over her fries. "We have to start now. Prom's a month away."

"I'll try cherries so I can wear pink," Ashley says.

"My dress is blue. Think it'll work with blueberries?" Brittany asks.

Ruth wipes hummus from her lip. "Maybe. Blueberries help prevent cancer."

"We don't care about cancer," Lily says. "We care about prom."

In the coming weeks, the girls stock up on fruit, all Norman brand except Ruth's. She's chosen Concord grapes like Lily. She'll replicate the experiment as close as she can to see if she can repeat the results. With herself as subject, she can take precise measurements and record symptoms. Only one problem. Her parents only buy organic produce, so the grapes are small and keep running out. Her little sister Kimmy gobbles them up. There's a store four miles away, but Ruth's bike is rusted. She needs grapes fast. Huge grapes. Bushels of grapes. Grapes by the truckload. The organic ones aren't working. Maybe the thing in grapes that boosts pheromones only works with grapes the size of a spoon. She needs to act quick.

She broaches the subject after dinner while her dad's making the grocery list.

"We need cornmeal," her mother says.

"Raspberry oatmeal bars," Kimmy adds.

With the pencil still moving, Ruth adds, "Concord grapes. And they have to be Norman. Make sure they're Norman, Dad. And get lots."

"Concord grapes it is." Her father pencils it in. "But Norman uses pesticides. You know that."

"They're the juiciest though. I read an article in *Healthy Living* that says they prevent blood clots and reduce the acidity in urine."

"That's *all* grapes," her mother says. "You can get the same benefits with organic."

"Not necessarily," Ruth answers. "Since Norman grapes are twice the size, that's twice the juice and flavonoids and vitamin C."

"You can eat twice as many organic grapes if you're concerned about your flavonoid intake," her father says. "We'll drive to the farmer's market this weekend."

"But those grapes are tiny."

"Norman isn't organic," her mother says, rising to clear the dishes.

"So?" Ruth replies. She's heard Lily use this retort.

"So, our daughters don't eat pesticides," her mother answers. "End of story."

"You'd rather I eat bugs?" Ruth asks. Usually, she doesn't test her parents, but this time passivity isn't an option. "I'm serious," she says. "I'm sick of eating fruit covered in insects." She slams her fork on the table. It bounces onto the floor.

"You'll eat the food we buy or nothing," her father says. "*That's* final."

"I hate that organic shit," Ruth says.

"That's enough," her mother says. "You just got yourself a week of dish duty." She tosses the dishcloth on the table, lifts Kimmy from her booster seat, and heads upstairs.

"I'm taking a shower," her father says.

"Fuck," Ruth whispers. She picks up the cloth with two fingers. Soapy water drips. She slops it back on the table and pushes the suds around.

The dishes done, Ruth heads upstairs and finds Kimmy in her room trying to stuff the head on a My-Little-Pony. "Give it here," Ruth says. She swivels the head into place. "Wanna color?" Ruth asks. Coloring is quiet, and she isn't in the mood to talk. Kimmy selects a Transformers coloring book, and Ruth sits by the window that faces the Prestons' driveway. A decade ago, Felix's dad nailed a basketball hoop to the garage before he left town. In the years since, Felix hasn't missed a night out at the hoop. Ruth braids Kimmy's hair, reads stories, plays ponies, anything to watch from her bedroom. She likes the way his wrists flip as the ball leaves his hands. She pulls the curtains back and watches him line up a shot.

Ruth and Lily played once with Felix when they were eight. Ruth imagines that day repeating: Felix's arms stretched to block her, his breath on her skin.

Since then, the closest she's gotten is the time he dyed his hair green. He filled a washbasin with concentrated lemon-lime Kool-aid, set it on the porch steps and leaned his nest of bleached hair back to soak. When Ruth and Lily stepped over him, he grabbed Ruth's ankle.

"What do you say we turn your hair green too, little girl?" he said.

Ruth froze, his hand digging into her skin.

"Right," Lily said. "Green hair on a girl who won't even get layers."

Ruth wanted to prove Lily wrong. Lily hated her brother. He told his friends she had STDs. He didn't want her crashing his parties. But they had each other on blackmail. Lily kept quiet about the pot, the beer, the parties, and Felix didn't tell their mother about Lily's reputation, the boys, the sex. Ruth commiserated with Lily in private. She'd say, "You're right. He's a jerk. You should put termites in his sneakers." But sometimes she did his homework. And that day, she almost switched sides. She wanted him to hold her leg forever. She wanted him to dye her hair green. But then Lily grabbed her hand, and Ruth conceded. She wriggled away and followed her friend into the house. Now she watches Felix from her sister's window. It's a secret she keeps from Lily, a small deception that reminds her Lily doesn't always win.

"You're not coloring," Kimmy says.

Ruth lets go of the curtain and rips back the paper on an orange crayon. Over her sister's head, she sees Felix flip the ball into the air. The green curls of his hair lift as his body rises. They fluff out and fall like wings.

Ruth knocks on the Prestons' door. Nobody answers, so she lets herself in. "Lily?" she calls. "Lily, it's me." She hears music through the ceiling.

Saturday mornings, Lily's always in one of two places. Either on her mother's bed watching *Brady Bunch* reruns. Or in her room with the music blaring, door locked. If she's watching TV, Ruth scooches up on the bed beside her. If she's in her room, Ruth waits her out and cleans.

The mess at the Prestons' is always a little bit shocking, so different from Ruth's house, where nothing is ever amiss. As a rule, the girls have to march all their belongings—flashcards, bug collections, bead looms—up to their rooms at night. Their family motto is "Never go to bed with a messy house," while the motto at Lily's seems to be, "Why do the dishes if a clean dish is left? And maybe not even then." When Lily's family runs out of dishes, they use paper plates. When those are gone, they use napkins, then the least dirty dish in the sink.

Ruth makes a game of collecting dishes from all over the house. She likes rubbing Brillo pads over sticky surfaces to make them shiny, rinsing dishes and stacking them tall. Standing at the sink with suds to her elbows, she feels she belongs in this house. And in the hour it takes to clean the kitchen, Felix often stops by for food.

Today, she has a plan and starts with the fridge. She turns over bags of moldy carrots. She looks behind beer cans and soda, a pizza box, pickles. No fruit. Ruth takes out cartons and jugs. She imagined the fridge would be bursting with grapes. Ruth opens the pickles and pops one into her mouth.

"Don't your parents feed you?" It's Felix.

She whips around. "Just cleaning," she says, with pickle still on her tongue. "Fridges are one of the filthiest places." She grabs the moldy carrots. "See." Cloudy liquid drips from the bag.

"Awesome," he says.

Ruth drops the carrots into the trash. They hit with a thud.

Felix snatches bread from the breadbox, a knife from the sink. "Turkey still good?"

"I think." She hands him cold cuts, provolone, the jar of mayonnaise. "The cheese might be bad. It's past the expiration date."

Felix slops mayo on the bread, smacks the pieces together, and rips a bite with his teeth. "Delicious," he says, and grabs his keys from the counter, heads out the door, then stops. "You don't have to do that, you know."

"I like to," Ruth says.

He shrugs. "Suit yourself."

"You going to the store?" she asks. "I have money." She pulls out a five-dollar bill.

"That'll only get you a six pack."

"I need grapes. Concord Norman," she says. "You can keep the change."

"There's a mess of them in Lily's room," he says. "Go on up. She's got a mini-fridge."

"Lily doesn't share," Ruth replies.

"Some friend," he says, and takes the bill from her hand. "If I remember." He slips it into his pocket and leaves. She watches his car shoot down the driveway, the sandwich wedged in his mouth.

Above her, the music pauses. Ruth tosses Felix's knife in the sink and heads upstairs. But before she can get there, the music's pounding again. She tries Lily's knob. Locked. But Felix's door is open. She pokes her head into his room. Black walls, black carpet, even black sheets heaped on a mattress on the floor, pictures of naked women taped to the ceiling, basketball posters tacked to the walls. A stack of *Playboys* is beside the mattress. She picks one up and leafs through. A piece of paper is tucked in back. A list of names, Lily's on top, Brittany, Claire and Ashley down a bit farther. Ruth's at the bottom, second from last. Beside the names are letters and numbers. Ruth knows the dates, their birthdays. And the initials are easy. B.L. Bobby Litchfield. J.A. Josh Anthony. But why the S's? Satisfactory? Smart? Slutty?

"What the fuck are you doing?"

Ruth spins around. "Phew, you scared me. Check this out." She hands Lily the paper.

She shrugs. "Guys rank girls all the time. So they think I'm hot and you're not."

"But the letters." Ruth points to the S next to Lily's name. "It seems like a code."

"Sexy," Lily says.

"Then why do they need our birthdays?"

Lily shrugs. "Only lesbos look at *Playboy.*"

She goes to the bathroom and slams the door. Ruth hears water pounding the tub. She reads the list again. At the end: Ruth Hammond 7/17/98. Her birthdate is almost a year before Lily's. She started kindergarten ahead. Then more initials. F.P. Felix Preston. Her chest flutters. There's a V beside her name. Vegetarian? Valedictorian? No, V is for virgin, of course. Maybe Felix would date her if he knew she'd put out. Maybe he's worried about her age. She won't be eighteen for another four years. She couldn't legally have sex with him until then.

Two weeks before prom, the girls sit in the cafeteria, slightly tinted zombies. The color's subtle. They have to turn just the right way in just the right light. Claire's pink. Ashley orange. Brittany asphyxiation blue. And Lily's got lavender lips. Ruth, by contrast, is still pale and chalky like everyone else at their school. Plus, she's the only one at the table without a date for prom. Her friends have swept up the basketball team's starting line, all except Felix, who Lily says is holding out for the best piece of ass.

"It's funny the fruit only attracts athletes," Ruth puzzles. "All from the same sport and all from the senior team. Have the boys in *our* class been flirting?"

"Why would we want ninth-grade boys?" Lily asks.

"I'm just saying. If it's the fruit, shouldn't all the boys be flocking?"

"Don't think too hard," Lily says. "You'll break a sweat. Boys don't like pit stains."

"Or BO," Ashley pipes in.

Ruth bites a celery stick and sighs.

"You're just cranky you don't have a date," Lily says. "Sucks for you. Not for us." Lily hoists a cluster of grapes in the air and clinks them against Ashley's orange for a toast. "Three cheers for yours truly," she says. "If not for me, none of you would have made it to prom before high school. I should get an award."

"We've thanked you plenty," Claire says, sucking a cherry.

Brittany pops a blueberry into her mouth. "My sister went to five proms. My goal is to hit double digits."

"But there's only one a year," Ruth says.

"Only one at Crow Hill, retard," Lily says. "There are proms all over the country."

Ruth goes back to her hummus sandwich. Maybe it's not the pheromones, she thinks. Maybe it's like all those turn-of-the-century tubercular women who men found gorgeous because they looked fragile and sick. Maybe basketball players like their girls diseased.

Lily waves a yellow slip of paper. "Who else got one of these?"

The other girls pull theirs from their pockets and line them up on the table.

"I guess a trip to the guidance office is in order," Lily says. "Miss Michaels probably wants to give us her 'no means no' talk."

"I thought it was 'cause I flunked Spanish," Claire says.

Brittany says, "I thought she was pissed I skipped gym."

"It's about prom," Lily says. "Mr. Henrik sends Miss Michaels the list of people going. She's probably worried we'll get raped. We'll go sixth period. Ruth, you're coming too."

"I didn't get a note," Ruth says. "I've got AP Earth Science."

"Tough shit," Lily says.

"Why her?" Ashley asks.

"Teachers love Ruth," Lily says. "Look at that face. No one would think to rape her."

When Ruth gets home from school, there are four bags of grapes on the steps. Concord grapes busting out of the plastic and huge like eggs. He remembered, she thinks. And this feels like a triumphant thing. She bangs open the door and drops her backpack. She skips with her grapes to the kitchen, spritzes them with vegetable cleaner, and rinses them off. She pours them into a Coleman cooler and plops one on her tongue. She'll eat one bag now and save the rest. She plans to slice some thin to make into slides. At school, she can look for abnormal cells under the microscope. But now the house is empty. And she's got a bag of grapes to herself.

She heads upstairs with the cooler and climbs out the bathroom window onto the roof. She leans against the house, letting the brick warm her back. She can see into Lily's room. But it's empty. She sinks down under a canopy of leaves and rolls a grape on her tongue. A folded pamphlet in her back pocket pokes her. She shifts her hips to retrieve it. It's the bulimia pamphlet Miss Michaels gave her. Ruth reads the words in bold: BINGING, PURGING, LAXATIVE USE. She told Miss Michaels she didn't do these things. The other girls got pamphlets on anorexia. Miss Michaels said they were pale and hadn't been eating much at lunch. She told them if they didn't eat enough, their hair and teeth would fall out, and their brains would rot. Lily kicked Ruth under the table, and Ruth spoke up. "Actually, Miss Michaels," she said. "We've all been eating healthy meals with lots of fruit since fruit stimulates the intestinal muscles and absorbs nutrients into our blood."

Miss Michaels smiled, said, "Ruth, I know you're eating. But I'm worried about your friends. Girls your age should eat two thousand calories a day."

Ashley snickered. Brittany stifled a laugh. Ruth watched Lily's chin tremble. She'd seen this before. When the community players did *The Crucible*, Lily got the lead because she could cry on cue. When asked how she did it, Lily said she imagined how her friends would feel if she died. It started with that quiver in her chin. Then she sniffled and wiped her nose with her hand. Miss Michaels handed over a tissue. "I feel misled," Lily said. "When the nutritionist came this winter, she told us to eat boatloads of fruit. She kept saying 'an apple-a-day,' and we figured why not two or five or eight?"

Her voice broke apart, and she started to cry. Miss Michaels touched her knee. "It's not that fruit is bad," she said. "But you have to eat more than that."

"You don't understand," Lily mumbled. "I just want to be pretty. The boys are always staring, and I feel so ugly."

"Oh, honey," Miss Michaels said. "You're not ugly. Not even close."

"Don't try to make me feel better," Lily said. "I know I'm hideous. I feel like a midget. No, a leper." A tear lingered on her cheek.

Ruth stood, and her chair hit the floor. "If you're a leper, I'm a mongoose," she said. "And this mongoose is going back to class."

Now Ruth wonders if Lily is mad. She knows Lily didn't need her at Miss Michaels's office. She just wanted to prove that despite Ruth's brains, Lily ran the show. But Ruth was the one who had found the *Chic* article. She didn't even get credit for that. She crumples the bulimia pamphlet, and stuffs a grape in her mouth. She bites, and juice slides down her throat. She lets the next one sit on her tongue. It presses against her lips. She turns another one in her hand. Then with a fingernail, peels back the skin and sets a scrap of it on her palm. It seems normal. She examines the veins on its flesh. She peels more skin, uncurls the purple film on her hand. Dark juice pools into the creases. She licks it. It tastes like fruit. But her palm stays purple. She licks it again and checks her tongue. The tip of her tongue is stained. Deep, dark, almost black. Grapes don't dye your tongue, she thinks. Not like that. Could they have dyed the fruit? She'd heard about oranges being dyed, the peel infused with color, but never grapes.

The light flicks on in Lily's room, and Ruth ducks behind the tree. She wipes her hands on her jeans and watches Lily take her dress out of the closet. Lily rips off her shirt and jeans, wiggles the dress over her head, adjusts the cups. She struts, watching herself in the mirror. The gown is violet and crisscrosses in back. Below the straps, the dress scoops down, showing the hollow groove of her spine. And for a moment with purple seeping into her tongue, Ruth forgets to bite or swallow or breathe.

Miss Michaels sends letters to the girls' parents, saying they need to watch their daughters' diets. Their parents make them eat balanced meals. At school, the girls mourn the loss of the fruit that made their skin glimmer radiant colors. All but Ruth. Ruth is ebullient. Her parents didn't get a letter. Miss Michaels doesn't think Ruth has bulimia, not even that. They think she's so good and sweet. But the joke's on them.

She's eaten nothing but grapes for a week. She and Felix have a deal. Ten bags of grapes on her steps every Thursday. Money in his locker. In exchange, she writes his essays for the rest of the year. To avoid her parents' watchful eyes she told them she needs to stay late at school until the science fair to prep for the state competition. She gets rides home with Mrs. Keller who lives across the street and teaches aerobics in the gym. Ruth's mom saves her a plate of food, and Ruth dumps it under the compost. When her parents go to bed, she blends the Norman grapes with water and food coloring. She sips it through a straw and scrubs her tongue before bed.

No one suspects. And already she senses a change. If only she wasn't behind. The other girls have been eating fruit two weeks longer. And although their parents make them eat chicken and broccoli at home, their skin still glows with the complexion of berries. Plus, they've already got dates for prom. Ruth is afraid the grapes won't work their magic by then. Prom's less than a week away, and it's all the talk.

"What color do you think my corsage will be?" Claire asks on the way to gym.

"I dunno," Lily says. "Let's ask."

They detour through the cafeteria. The lunchroom is already decorated with balloons and streamers. The boys count a stack of twenty-dollar bills.

"How much you got there, boys?" Lily asks, her pack of slightly faded girls by her side. "Better be two or three hundred. I'm worth that much at least."

"Why would they give you money?" Ruth asks.

Felix hits Bobby's shoulder. "Dude, you told her?"

Bobby shrugs and grabs Lily. "Coming for some pregame action?" he asks.

Felix kicks him under the table. "Knock it off, ass wipe."

"Claire wants a red corsage," Lily announces.

"I want blue," Brittany says.

"You get what you get," Felix replies.

Ruth watches him eat spaghetti goulash with his hands. The tips of his fingers are greasy orange. He glares at his sister. "Shouldn't you and your posse be in class?"

"We have gym," Ruth says.

"Ah, gym," Felix says. He brushes green hair from his forehead and licks his fingers. "What about you?" he asks. "You going to prom?"

Lily snickers.

"Not exactly," Ruth says.

"If you're interested," Felix says, "limo comes at seven."

"Me?" Ruth asks, her cheeks turning red. "You want me to go?"

Lily glares at her brother. "She's your trump card? Trust me, that won't pan out."

"Carnations okay?" Felix asks.

"Carnations are cheap," Lily says. "I'm glad my date doesn't eat with his hands." She sulks out of the cafeteria, her flip-flops hitting the floor with angry slaps.

The girls follow her into the hall. "I don't believe he asked you to prom," Ashley says.

"Well," Ruth answers. "We are neighbors."

"Do you have a dress?" Brittany asks.

"You know you have to wear a thong, right?"

"I wonder why he asked you," Claire says. "You haven't been eating Norman fruit."

"Actually, I have," Ruth says.

The bell rings, and they hurry to gym. Lily and Ruth have lockers in the same row. Ruth turns her dial to thirty-four, then two full times around to the left. "You don't mind, do you?" she asks.

"Why should I care?" Lily says. She rips her bra over her head and glances at her A-cup breasts in the mirror. Her nipples are purple. She pulls a sports bra over her head and shoves her feet into sneakers.

"I don't know," Ruth says. "You just seem upset."

"Not at all," Lily says. "It's just—I didn't expect you'd want to go."

"Why?" Ruth asks. She turns toward her locker to change her shirt.

"You've never even kissed a guy, Ruth. You know Felix expects you to suck his dick."

"Just because that's all you think about, doesn't mean he's like that," Ruth says.

"You're right. My brother's a goddamn prince."

Lily slams her locker and turns around. "Why do you think Claire and Ashley are going? You think Brittany's suddenly hot because her earlobes are blue? There's a bet to see which basketball player can get blown by the youngest prom date. You saw the list."

"Then why would you go?"

"Because I like to win."

The conversation runs through Ruth's head the rest of the day. When Señorita Gonzales asks, "¿Como se dice *potatoes* en Español?" Ruth almost says *penis*.

After school, she skips her work in the lab and goes home to practice on a banana. Drool drips down her chin. She thinks about it all night. Doing homework, she sticks herself with a pen. Taking the compost out, she walks into the screen door. She calls Felix and cancels their date. She says her grandfather's diabetic, and the doctors have to cut off his feet. She'll be at the hospital all weekend. She can't go to prom. "Maybe next year," she says.

"Whatever," he says, and hangs up.

Ruth wonders if he'll tell Lily. She knows Ruth's grandfathers are dead. She dials the Prestons' number. Maybe she could say she was joking. As soon as it rings, she hangs up. She runs upstairs to the bathroom to see if Felix is in Lily's room, spreading the news. She shoves open the door. Her mother's in the tub.

"Oh, sorry. I just need floss," Ruth says. But she doesn't turn away from her mother's breasts, the wide areolas the color of plums.

"Since you're here, you can grab me the razor."

Ruth snatches it from the sink and hands it over. Then she rifles in the medicine cabinet.

"Floss is in the drawer," her mother says.

"Oh yeah," Ruth says. She wraps a piece around her fingers. In the mirror, she watches her mother soap her legs. "I got asked to prom this year," she says. "By a junior."

"Oh?" her mother says, not looking up.

"I told him I couldn't go. Since it's so close to AP exams."

"Isn't there a freshman dance at the end of the month?"

"That one's lame," Ruth says. "No one goes." She weasels the floss between her molars. "Lily's going to prom," she says. "I feel bad ditching her."

"I hope Sharon's talked to her daughter about sex."

"They cover that at school," Ruth says. "Every year."

Ruth drops her floss in the trash. She goes to the window and parts the blinds. Lily's room is dark.

"Maybe when Lily hears you're not going, she'll change her mind," her mom says. "Proms are disappointing. You girls could have a sleepover instead."

"She already bought her dress," Ruth says. "But I'll tell her." She lets go of the blinds. "Gotta do homework," she says, and scampers down the hall.

In her room, she turns on her laptop and searches Google. She always finds answers online. She scans an article about fruit dye's effects on mice. An ad for citrus gift baskets. Then bingo. A wholesale catalogue of juice and wine supplies. Under food additives, vials of dye. She uses her mom's emergency credit card to order, checks OVERNIGHT SHIPPING. Then, ORDER NOW. And bing. A purple complexion in a bottle. Lily would never think of that.

Two days later, a package comes in the mail. A shoebox size. Ruth sneaks it up to her room and rips through the paper. Packing peanuts spill out with four vials of dark purple dye. She divides them up. Three days until prom. One a day. One that night. She will be purple whether or not she goes. Prom's not about the actual dance, she thinks. It's about how you look in the pictures. She can join her friends at the after-party next door. When they see her skin, they will know that Ruth can do magical things.

She stays home the last two days of the school week. A migraine, she says. Her mother tells her she's working too hard, and Ruth solemnly nods her head. Alone in the house, she sips diluted dye, and pees lavender streams.

The Saturday of prom, she stays in bed most of the day. She studies AP notes, does shots of purple dye, and scrubs her tongue. Her mother checks her temperature before bed. "I feel much better," Ruth says. "I got lots of studying done."

Her mother kisses her head. "You look a bit blue," she says.

Ruth smiles. "Probably just the light."

When her parents' room goes dark, Ruth sneaks downstairs and finds an old bridesmaid dress in Kimmy's costume box. It's magenta and dotted with sparkling stones. Her mother wore it in a wedding. Ruth pulls up her hair and paints her nails. She waits on the porch roof for the limo to return from the dance. She eats the last of her grapes. A week's worth of antioxidants stir inside her, and her tongue is numb from the sweetness of their juice.

She watches Lily step out of the car first. The light from the moon turns her arms an ethereal blue. Felix helps Jenna Hayes climb out. Ruth knows her from band. That could have been me, she thinks, if not for Lily. Lily knew the blowjob thing would freak her out. Ruth watches Lily go into the house, her shoes tucked under her arm. When she comes back, she's wearing flip-flops and carrying wine coolers, two per hand.

By midnight, the Prestons' lawn is filled with cars. Girls turn cartwheels. Their skirts billow over their heads.

Ruth watches her friends on the Prestons' porch. She stays out of sight. Brittany and Claire sing Hannah Montana songs. Lily leans against a pillar, with a crate of grapes at her feet. She dangles fruit over her mouth, bites off three in a row. She washes them down with wine cooler, a berry blend. "Fuck a balanced diet," she says. "By morning I'll be purple again."

"Where'd the boys go?" Brittany asks. "Maybe I should look for Blake."

"So you can fuck him?" Lily says.

"Maybe."

"He left an hour ago in Shannon Murphy's car."

"That skank." Brittany throws an empty bottle into the grass.

"She rented a hotel suite," Lily says. "Jenna and April went too."

"Help me find Josh," Claire says, and drags Brittany up. Brittany grabs Ashley's hand and the three of them link arms.

"I'm staying here," Lily says. "Bobby went for beer. I'm watching out."

The girls skip away, and Lily stares at the lavender spheres of her nails. Ruth's been waiting to catch her alone. She wants to tell Lily she got it wrong, to say she's not afraid of blowjobs. She's not a naïve little twerp who Lily can boss around. She pulls up her dress, slings a leg over the tree, and climbs down.

When Lily sees her, she smiles. "Ruth, where have you been? You missed it. It's over. You don't need to dress up now."

"I came to see you," Ruth says. "Look what I did." She holds out her arms.

"It's makeup," Lily says. "You didn't have time to do it for real."

"Go ahead. Try to rub it off. I ordered Norman dye. You're not the only one with tricks."

Lily shrugs. "What does it matter now? You don't have a date. We're out of boys." Lily sinks her teeth into a grape the size of an eyeball. "Oh wait. You came for me." She laughs and spits grape on the ground. "I saw you on the roof. I know you watch me. I know you didn't go to prom with Felix because you want me instead." Lily stands, but her dress catches her toe. She hits the ground, and her skirt flips over her thigh. Ruth can see her underwear. Lavender with little blue moons and stars.

"Lily, your panties are showing. Lily, get up."

Lily grabs Ruth by the ankle. "Not 'till you kiss me."

"I came to see Felix."

"Bullshit," Lily says. "You came for me."

"Let go," Ruth says. She tries to shake Lily off, but she holds on tighter. Ruth drags her toward the porch. She kicks her leg and wrangles free.

"Don't leave," Lily cries from the grass. "Ruthie, I feel so sick."

"You shouldn't have had wine coolers," Ruth scolds. "Sugar induces nausea." She grabs Lily under the armpits and pulls her to the steps. "Lean over your knees," she says. "Take deep breaths. How many bottles did you drink?"

"A lot," Lily says.

Ruth wipes grass off Lily's cheek and feels her pulse.

"I know you love me," Lily says. She pushes her lips against Ruth's. Her lips are soft and tinged with the sweetness of grapes. Ruth kisses her back.

"I knew it," Lily says, breaking away. "You're a lesbo. Wait 'till I tell the girls."

"You started it," Ruth says.

"I was just testing."

"I could tell Bobby."

"Go ahead," Lily says. "He would love . . ." She laughs and chokes on a burp. Ruth hears vomit rise in Lily's throat. She swallows it and slides to the ground. She curls up in the grass, and her hair falls in the dirt. "I'm tired," she says.

"You can't sleep," Ruth says. "That's the worst thing you could do."

Lily smiles. "I can do whatever I want."

Ruth props her up on the porch and slaps her cheek. Lily tries to push her away. Ruth takes Lily's chin in her hand and uses her mother's voice. "Listen to me, Lily Marie Preston. You're going to sit here just like this and stay awake until I come back with water and food."

In the kitchen, the refrigerator shelves are filled with beer. The grapes feel heavy in Ruth's stomach. A pain shoots through her head. She shifts beer cans from side to side, searching for food. Usually the fridge is full of take-out containers. She'll take anything. Pizza. Eggrolls. Noodles. She finds half a sub and rips off the foil. She smells turkey and mustard. She bites through the bun. She hasn't eaten solid food in a week. The flavors feel good in her mouth. She stands in the light of the fridge and chews.

"You want something, little girl?" She jumps. Felix stands in the doorway. He's not wearing shoes.

"Lily's drunk. I'm getting her something to eat."

"Testing to see if it's spoiled?"

Ruth swallows the mush in her mouth. "I should get back. She didn't look good. You guys have crackers?"

"She's blacked out before," he says. He takes the sandwich from her hand and sets it on the counter. "You don't have to take care of her."

"She's my friend," Ruth says.

"Right," Felix says. He takes her hand and licks her finger. "Mmm. Mustard." He licks it again. "How come you never have any fun?"

"I do," Ruth says. "I—" Then Felix's mouth is on her lips. Ruth breathes through her nose. He smells like beer and cigarettes. When he lets go, Ruth unclenches her toes. Felix takes her hand and leads her into the other room. He sinks into the couch and pats the cushion beside him. He's still wearing the pants from his tux. A white T-shirt on top. "Sit," he says.

Ruth crouches on the edge of the cushion. She looks around the room. "Where's Jenna?" she says.

"I sent her home. She's kinda dumb." He slides close. "You gotta tell me," he says. "Did they cut off his feet?"

"What?" she asks.

"Your grandpa. I've been wondering. When they did it, when they cut off his feet, how did they stop the blood?" He presses his lips to hers again. Their teeth hit. She feels his tongue. "You ever touch one?" he asks. He takes her hand and guides it through his zipper. Her fingers course through wiry hair. Ruth feels the warmth of his body. He pushes his pants to the floor, rips his shirt over his head. Ruth stares. He has the same pale stomach as Lily, the same belly button popping out like a knob. Ruth stares at his penis, erect and angled. She didn't think it would look like that. He takes her hand and wraps her fingers around it, guides her up and down. The skin rolls and stretches. He moans softly and clutches her arm. "There you go," he says. "Now lick the tip."

Ruth does as he says. She presses his penis to her lips and sucks gently, caressing the flesh with her tongue.

Outside the noise of the party gets louder. Ruth looks out the window. She hears sirens. A bottle breaking. A car door slamming shut.

Felix grips her arm tighter. "Don't stop," he says. His fingers dig into her skin.

Ruth brings his penis to her mouth. Over his shoulder, she sees Lily in the doorway. Red lights flash behind her. She's biting her lip. Ruth knows that look. It's the look she gets on her face before she cries. Ruth holds her breath, closes her eyes, and lets the sirens fill her head.

opal one,
opal two

━━━━━

opal one—insect smallness, brown-gray girl, who scurries on spindly legs. so busy crossing empty spaces, sometimes she doesn't breathe. thus the miniature hiccups. staccato sounds that lurch from her throat. pinprick hiccups. and pit pit patters, raindrop feet pocking patterns on the floor. little daughter. watch her flutter. little daughter. watch her twirl. she darts. she spins in circles. so pretty when she's flitting. a blur of brown-gray limbs that look like wings. but when she sleeps, her features crumple. eyes and nose so close together. forehead furrowed. wrinkled chin. scrunched little face like a moth. edda thinks opal is more ruby's daughter than hers.

edda—sews seams with the sight of her fingers. sews robes for all the priests. for prayer. for choir. for blessing water in baths of birds. edda with thread spinning under her fingers. toes tapping the pedal that powers the lever, that moves thread through the needle. the needle sharp. the needle thin. all that sewing, and opal always whisking away. past the edges of edda's glasses. to the peripheral fog of muddy eyes. such frenzy. like edda's sister ruby. whose voice was always zip zip zipping. throat erupting with words. a pulse that buzzed in edda's ears. and only ceased when ruby took glass on her tongue. melting it with her breath. the vaulted roof of her mouth bending it round. unlatch the lips. to release the rose-colored lens. that mends the muddy eyes. that colors the world. until the glass outlives its time. and the eyes get muddier still.

father babcock—singing his way through all the hymnals. kneeling in pew number eight. the singing such work he's split a seam in his robe. the flesh of his elbow pokes through. he sings to sister maurice who rubs oil into the alter. he sings to crucified jesus. and one-dimensional mary, piecemeal, soldered with lead, spider line crack splitting her face in two. three sheep on a hill behind her. the sun intersects the hill, shines green on the bald of his head. a cap like peter pan. all he needs is a feather. bathed in the green of the window. singing a string of hallelujahs. a moth cries for help in the rafters. he looks but can't find it in all the wood.

opal one—fond of the big machine's rumble. purring needle. warm light from its tiny sun. when she comes close to her mother's fingers, edda blows at her shadow and opal is swept away, suspended on breath from her lungs. whisked to the window. where two little girls excavate worms from the dirt. opal might like to uncork a worm from the ground herself. but she is not a sister. so she stays inside and goads the needle. with her nine-hundred thread-count flesh. today too close. the tip of the needle catches her skirt. leg stitched into the seam, sewn into the robe. dark in the crease of the hem. ecclesiastical velvet, a mask that muffles her tongue. saliva leaks into velvet. cloth transposes to moss under her head.

edda—furious whir of the needle. manic winging of opal's legs. the buzzing resurrects ruby. ruby five years dead. poor ruby. glass in her lungs, shards splintering into her blood. remember ruby clenching her fists. remember ruby pursing her chin. everything tight because everything hurt. because glass was etching her insides, burrowing into her organs. little razors under her skin. but edda didn't believe her, told her to stop her clenching or she'd grind her teeth to nubs. she was always shushing her sister. saying still those pulsing lips. now no sister to shush. only snot erupting from nostrils. spittle caught on her tongue. sogginess steams her lenses. and she doesn't see opal under her fingers. hear the thread knot. hear the cloth catch. then in the silence. the wind through the window. a bird in the mulberry tree.

antoinette—mud. mud. mud. squishy squish in the hands. scrippity scrape on the legs. sands the bump of the elbow. rubs fur from little girl arms. softens the skin. eases the itch. covers sister's rosy smell. rosy sister squeals, keep the dirt to yourself. so dirty sister does. mud on the worms instead. worms weave through the tines of her fingers. stretch over her palms like cello strands. their bellies smooth on her cheek. the pentamerous beating of hearts seeps into her skin, does jigs on her tongue. where's opal? dirty sister needs a partner to dance to the rat tat tat of the worms. gone from the window. nobody's sister. drop a worm in the jar for opal. opal dances alone.

edda—tangles and knots under her fingers. the pit pit patter gone. floor space quiet. except the breath of the dust. everything still like rubble. except the bird perched in the mulberry tree. spreading her wings. puffing the fringe of her throat. hysterical chirping. manic scissoring beak. tizzied creature. like opal. dear god. where's opal? has opal turned into this bird? oh ruby. sad suffering sister. edda's comeuppance earned. come back, edda calls to opal. the tree shifts its branches. the bird startles, leaps out of the tangle. the sky swallows her up. edda lurches. thinks exit. but her leg is snagged in velvet, velvet caught under the chair. her cheek slams to the floor. rose-colored lenses splinter. eyes begotten by ruby. bowed by the might of her tongue. a shower of rose-colored seeds disperses. color leaks from the world. and edda escapes the house.

opal one—mother crashing down. mother gone the house. opal all alone. hung from a weave of scalloped threads. stitches pierce her toes and cuff her bones to the cloth. lick the dark cocoon. lap the velvet smooth. fed on the juice of the tongue, velvet blooms into moss. mossy meadows creep. over brown-gray skin. and weasel under her arms and wrap wreaths around her womb. hold the daughter tight. rock the daughter still. cup mossy hands to her eyes, but leave the ears unblocked. let her listen to the rattle of rose-colored seeds. shells split open, and seeds let loose a chorus of tiny screams.

helen—shaking a jar of worms. the glass blurs pink with skin. antoinette holds the spoon that does the digging. antoinette with dirt on her tongue. dirty sister. wash her down with the hose. then tack her to the clothesline. hung by her dirty hair. dirty sister points to edda. edda rushing down the road. to see the jar of worms. is that opal? she asks the children. antoinette shakes her head no. edda looks at the sisters. exactly the same. except one holds a jar of skin to her chest, and the other holds fistfuls of dirt to hers. helen leads, and antoinette follows. they walk and edda goes too. quick little heel-to-toe steps. a parade marching. cobbled road to cobbled church.

father babcock—such a day. a moth lost in the rafters. edda's opal lost in the clouds. terrible trouble. what to be done. first, the abducted girl. ripped though a tear in the sky. send sister maurice to staple it shut. then rip a hymn from the hymnal. the one illogically transposed. too many sharps to be sung. scribble message to minor angel. SEND SECOND DAUGHTER. SEND SOON. fold into a bird. set out on the wind. such work, clerical robe splits up the back. never mind. the sewing's halted. light a candle instead. now bless the fretful mother. bless the jar of worms. and also this: the dirt on dirty sister's tongue.

edda—home again, but no opal. rose-colored seeds sprout rose-colored fruit on the floor. velvet rots to moss on the table. moss spills from metal mouth of broken machine. moss covered needle. moss covered thread. everything tangled. gather it up in a bundle. stow it away in the cedar chest at the foot of ruby's old bed. chest filled with lace. dowry for damaged daughters. one with muddy eyes. the other with glass in her lungs. lace knit with delicate fingers. fanatical mother. who knit with the bones of birds. her thread the silk of spiders. so many harvested webs.

opal one—dark in the thick of the moss. cedar smell feeds belly noises. hushes hiccups. cedar seeps into her tongue. ruby's room with ruby's ghost. mother's voice through the wall. singing the hymn sent away with the bird. opal wriggles around in the moss. moss holds tight to her leg. flexes her toes. reaches her hands through the lichen. gathers fistfuls of lace buried below. pattern of knots in her fingers. grandmother's worries like braille on her skin. worried the birds will forget the maps inked in their cerebellums. the clouds slip from their perches. moths knock their spines apart butting against the moon. so many worries wear opal out. smell of cedar swaddles. dear opal. sleep long, sleep well.

helen—stars recite insomniac sermons. treetops moan from holding so many leaves. owls cooing to ivy. ivy tapping morse code messages into the brick. helen tiptoes through yards, avoiding pockets of space where language passes through darkness. looking for opals. white rocks with rainbows glittering under their skin. granite pebbles sprinkled in gardens. almost opal. the best she can get. pick the prettiest pebbles. put in pockets. bring to edda's stoop. leave them with other gifts: mulberry pie. basket of fruit. gold leaf bible. and something left by dirty sister. her arm unstitched, fist full of dirt.

edda—wakes with ache in her organs. crawls out of bed. feeds ache with rose-colored fruit from the floor. thinks of ruby. glass lungs and glass intestines. vessels of blood a lattice of crystal, brittle between her bones. icicle hair breaking off behind her. feet crumbling on cobbles. glass teeth raining out of her mouth. coffin a pile of shimmering shards. for days, edda watched over the corpse. stroking the shards of shiny sister. finger pricked, sliver of sister entered her blood. grew into a daughter. now the daughter lost. edda goes to the door. but no opal. just offerings. who else but the clouds? hurl pie and fruit and bible back. the sky gives guilty gifts. gather the pebbles. gather the arm with its fistful of dirt. good gifts, come inside and sit on opal's bed.

father babcock—heavy bellied clouds graze shadowed steeple. stones in churchyard shiver. buried bodies call father babcock out. buried bodies wearing church clothes. can't get church clothes wet. father babcock with wheelbarrow full of umbrellas. pinwheel colors. sister maurice helps wedge them into the ground. look, the graves wear little fedoras. little yarmulke caps. watch out, sister maurice. that cloud's dripping soupspoons. a fork hits father babcock's head. it's edda on the steeple. fists full of kitchen utensils. hurling cutlery at the clouds. a war on the thief that stole her daughter. a daughter made from velvet and glass and guilt. sister maurice, huddle under the yellow umbrella. keep close. we'll wait it out. a butter knife reels through the air, pierces the sky. gold leaf pages leak out of the clouds. catch one on your tongue. the gospel according to mark.

antoinette—gold leaf pages raining. raincloud raining fruit. dig faster, clumsy elbow. scoop harder, wrong-handed hand. the one-armed girl is saving the world. dirty girl, you better hurry. or the worms will drown in psalms. have to shovel them out. helen, hold the jar a little closer. helen, help dirty sister dig, soupspoon for a spade. two hands only holding. hardly helping. lazy girl. now too many psalms in the soil. pink worms bloat under the weight of the word. knock helen over the head. lazy sister, you let them drown. swollen worms split out of their skin. tackle selfish sister. scoop out her ear with the silver spoon. selfish sister lies in the grass and yelps. tell her, still those pulsing lips. blessed be dirty sister. so says the word of the worms. go forth, dirty sister. with helen's hearing hidden in a jar of muddled skin.

opal one—slumber slipping away. roused by a hum in her ear. grandmother's voice soft as steam. grandmother's voice thick as milk. opal's tongue so dry. she suckles the moss, pulls water from its plumes. there there, sweet girl. ruby's fingers in her hair, stroking her head. opal feels the glass in ruby's skin. little pointed stars. quills that prick the scalp. shush, ruby says to the stars. hush your burning glow.

father babcock—travels cobbled street. umbrella for a head. umbrella knocks away shiny missiles. protects the tattered robe. and sacerdotal crown. sabbatical leave from cobbled parish. to halt crusade of mournful mother. launched on odious clouds. father babcock stands on stoop, hand lifted to the door. paper bird falls through fingers. lands on jar at father's feet. jar with an ear cupped in a cradle of worms. look, it's solomon's bird with wisdom in his beak. father babcock reads the bit on its wing. bird advises, break the girls and share their holy skin. father babcock runs back to cobbled church. sounds the message from the bells. hailing christian mothers with fleshly daughters in their homes. split the bread of your wombs.

antoinette—waterlogged worms. entrails spilled through a rift in their seams. to mend: roll garbled flesh against softest stone. roll with the palm of the hand. roll until flesh is smooth. then drop them back in the dirt. you'll have to mend them alone. selfish sister sleeping. missing absent ear. no girls to help dirty sister repair the damage. all girls tucked in bed. nursing open wounds. mothers line the sidewalk. baskets on their arms. bringing gifts for grieving mother. unstitched from goodly daughters. stalwart soldiers, get used to phantom limbs.

edda—second daughter. laid out on opal's bed. pieces puzzled into a body. parts of goodly daughters. head of little lamb. stitch the parts together. fill the gaps with rose-colored fruit. fill the hollow space with pebbles and worms. stitch on eyebrows. stitch on dimples. drip honey into her mouth. kiss her downy forehead. hold her trembling hand. she is opal too.

opal one—sweetness seeps into ruby's room. crawls through keyhole. into cedar chest. smell of fruit clambers into nostrils, rouses opal. stirs the sap in her stomach. pricks the freckles on her tongue. so hungry she nibbles the robe. so hungry she bites the lace. she eats and she listens. quiet in the chest. the ghosts are sleeping. but there are nighttime sounds in the house. a clatter in the hallway.

a slanted rhythm. hobbled feet. the clunk of mistuned bones. not at all the delicate patter of opal's delicate feet.

opal two—seeds rattle in her belly. pebbles clink against her ribs. percussive girl on mismatched legs. she shambles over cobbles. limbs aligned at awkward angles. matted tufts of wooly hair. all the girls throw pebbles, opal flees. up and up. into the mulberry tree. perched aloft, she watches the clouds. remembers dirt trickling down her chest. remembers granite marbles in her fists. and also the heat of a mouth. grains of a tongue pressing glass. bleeding roseate swirls into its skin.

edda—opal in a tree. rose-colored fruit swelling through the house. clouds ogle second daughter. mother shoos away the clouds. ushers daughter down. come, help mother harvest fruit. pluck bulging berries from the stems. squeeze fruit in iron pot. feed fire. add honey. stir until juice leaks from your thumbs. ladle into teacups. serve to girls with missing parts. watch them gulp. juice dribbles down their chins. stack teacups into tower. carry tower into house. so much work, mending malcontented neighbors. wears on mishmash body. stresses newly anchored limbs. rose-colored sap seeps from stitching, sweetens seams, scents the house. rose-colored worry seeps into the pillows and stains the walls.

opal one—crowded in a box with grandmother's worries, ruby's ghost, mountain of moss. stiffness in the limbs. heaviness in the throat. moss for breakfast. lace for lunch. sounds of mother and daughter for dinner. indigestible bits harden to glass in the lungs.

father babcock—sunday sermon. parish full. mothers and damaged daughters, goodly glow around their heads. bonnets and capes hide missing pieces. munificent daughters, who give of themselves. take tiny sips of wine. melt the bread on the tongues. father babcock presses prayers into their foreheads. closes his eyes and feels their breath on his skin. his robe, a gauze of rips and tatters. a moth weaves in and out of the holes.

antoinette—paper bird lands on finger. chirps, where are the worms? how to explain. the worms couldn't be mended. all that rolling. squashed their little heads. chirps, where is sister? sister making bonnet to cover empty ear. sister doesn't speak to antoinette. chirps, do i look like a bird? antoinette shakes her head no. unfolds it wing by wing. a message: ROSE-COLORED HOUSE. TEA AT NOON. antoinette shakes off the dirt. puts on pretty dress. sews spoons to the hem. metal clinks against her knees. now she sounds like opal two. opal two can be her sister. they can clink and clack together. every day. through cobbled streets. go on, and clatter to her house. underfoot: the smoothness of stones. overhead: a flock of folded birds.

opal two—damaged girls, it's time for tea. edda's gone for honey. opal two passes the cups. the girls sit in a circle, skirts whispering at their knees. a one-legged girl pours tea into her hollow stub. the one beside her (noseless) blows steam away from her cup. antoinette goes tinkle tinkle. her spoons clink as she sips. earless sister scowls. swats at dirty sister. topples rose-colored platter from opal's hands. the cake goes splat. the platter splinters. rose-colored seeds disperse, fall at their feet, grow into fruit. earless sister hurls cake and fruit at opal. the others follow, and opal flees the room. pebbles knock in her belly. seeds rattle in her chest. antoinette chases opal, juice dripping from her lips. she rounds the corner. but opal's gone. which door hides the second sister? the right or the left?

edda—jar of honey in her hands. just in time for tea. but all the little girls are gone. except the one wearing spoons. rose-colored fruit drips from the ceiling. pink frosting splatters the walls. tea cups toppled. earl grey rivers run around archipelagos of crumbs. where's opal? edda asks. opal one or opal two? either, edda says. antoinette shrugs, and the spoons hit together like bells.

opal one—ruckus in the house. smashing plates. thumping feet. the door of ruby's room screeches and slams. now the rattle of mismatched limbs. a sliver of light at the top of the chest. the lid bangs shut, and a girl falls through the moss. slips through pockets of lace and ruby's ghost and grandmother's leftover thoughts. comes to rest by brown-gray sister's head. fingers touch her scrunched little face. knees collide with spidery legs. opal two licks her sister's skin. belly hungry for flesh. just a little bite. from the gauze of brown-gray wings.

So Many Wings

The hospital says to come quick. Mary Lou
jumps in the car, steps on the gas. She ignores stop signs, cross-
walks, curbs. Knocks the mirror off a Jeep and keeps going. Parks
in a fire zone. She gets there gasping, nose dripping salt on her
tongue, hair frizzing out of a polka-dot headband, breasts loose
in her shirt and sweaty against her ribs. She sets her palms on the
counter, fingers gripping the grain of the wood. His name trips
over her teeth and the nurse flips through papers and pauses, biting a tiny nip of skin from her lip. Mary Lou gets there, but he's
already dead.

Already dead. Mary Lou licks the words to taste them. The dy-
ing already over. He's not going to die again. Then a policewoman

with more words. Words that careen and spark in Mary Lou's head. His car heading north. An empty road. His car slipping out of its lane. Tires rumbling on grooves in the pavement. First the right wheels. Then the left. Then no more pavement to cling to. Just a car rolling over and over, the hood ornament leaving divots in the hillside, a piece of roof metal severing his arm. Then blood. A deluge of red. Red soaking into tan upholstery. Into violets and grass and dirt. And in the middle of all these words, Mary Lou thinks, I should tell her I'm not his wife. Instead, she asks about his hands.

She says, I know that he's dead, but he plays piano. Are his hands okay? The policewoman shifts her weight from hip to hip, says, His arm was severed at the elbow. Says, It must have been out the window. People like to feel wind on their skin. Not Chester, Mary Lou says. She knows how he hated breezes. They would get in his eyes and sting like chlorine and turn the white parts pink so he looked like he'd been crying for days. She says, He wouldn't have put his arm out the window. Because of the wind. The policewoman rubs at her knuckles. Hard to say, she says. Maybe he was checking his phone. Or a deer crossed his path. Maybe he fell asleep. Mary Lou shakes her head. Chester's the most cautious driver I know. The policewoman shrugs. A fluke, she says. An accident. I'm sorry. She hands over his wallet, his watch, his keys. Mary Lou looks at these things. And the policewoman adds, Your husband's car got towed to Mortinson's shop. And again Mary Lou knows she should confess that she's not his wife. Though it would be just like Chester not to change his emergency contact. He knew she'd come. So she doesn't say they called the wrong woman. Because ex-wives don't get to hold the wallet of the man who rolled down the hill. Or hear the missing parts of the story filled in with words like cotton batting. Words like *elbow, window, skin.*

Then the policewoman with one more word. *Body.*

And again Mary Lou's nose is running. She wipes the drips on her shirt. Okay, she says. The body. And wipes her nose again.

She follows a balding doctor, who wears scrubs that are toothpaste green. And under the scrubs, moccasin shoes that are soundless and muffle his steps. The pink linoleum is speckled like salami. Chester hated salami, but Mary Lou loves it. She used to eat it in bed, savoring the salt on her tongue, and he would hide under the covers until she brushed her teeth. Then when she kissed him, he'd say she still had salami breath, that the salami stench had soaked all the way down into the salami pink of her lungs.

At the corner, the pink tiles turn into gray ones. And she thinks how Chester liked to spell *gray* with an *e*. He said it gave the word a drizzly feeling. *Gray* with an *a* made the word seem fat and happy and that felt false. He used British spellings for other words too. He put an *ou* in *color*, spelled *somber* with an *re*. When they were married, it made her cringe. But now she's in a tiled room, hard corners, perfectly cubed. And *sombre* seems like it *should* be spelled with an *r*, then an *e*, not soft like *silver* with vowels that lift off the tongue but hard like *fire*, like *ochre*, like *whore*. Because the room is white like the surface of aspirin. Because the light sheds blue shadows. Because wires wind around metal frames. The curtains so stiff and the surfaces laminate shiny, fixtures fixed with a plastic gloss. And everything's so bright, Mary Lou's eyes don't linger on the bed or the body until the doctor says, I'll be right outside in the hall. Then he leaves, and she can't look at anything else. Just the body under a sheet. A sheet so thin the grid of threads has risen to the surface like fat floating in milk, like blood blisters, and swollen ink.

It doesn't seem possible—Chester, the sheet, the body. Such a death seems careless, and Chester wasn't that. He always checked his mirrors two or three times. Checked his mirrors and looked over his shoulder and wore his seatbelt tight. He'd measure the air in his tires, check the battery, oil, and brakes. And when he finally got on the road, he never drove fast. He knew how tires could slip on pavement slick with oil, wet with rain. Like the day they met—a day rupturing with rain. With visibility hindered, Chester let up on the gas. Mary Lou was in the car behind his. Her shoes let in water. She wanted to go home and soak in the tub. She was tired and riding his tail, and Chester got nervous and braked. Then they hit.

When he got out of the car, she was shocked to see a man in his twenties. He said he was sorry, even though she was the one driving crazy. He kept asking if she was okay, but it was he who looked shaken. He kept biting his pinkie, ripping into the pink of the nail. He stood on the curb with rain plastering hair to his forehead, and when she stepped into the street to examine her bumper, he said she was making him nervous. She might get clipped by a car. So she joined him on the curb, and he told her about a friend with a shop who could fix her bumper for cheap.

He gave her his card, white letters spelling CHESTER LAWRENCE, the letters set on matted black, piano keys stamped at the bottom, a piano for a pianist the size of a thumb. She asked what kind of music he played, imagined his hands lurching like a marionette's legs. But he said, No, and his eyebrows scrunched in that way she later would know meant so so sorry. Not a musician. And suddenly this image of his hands frantic and flying tucked itself in the back of her head. Not a pianist, but rather a piano tuner, and really in the end, she had more need of someone like that. So she called him that week and asked if he'd tune the piano at the nursing home where she worked. The keys had the off-kilter clunk of a piano being played underwater, and whenever a resident banged out a tune, Mary Lou cringed at the way the songs broke apart, the notes falling into baffled collisions. Because it was, after all, a piano they'd found on the side of the road, the mahogany gouged with claw marks, hammers exposed, and many of the key covers gone, leaving gaps like missing teeth—

And now Mary Lou is thinking about body parts missing, and she loses her breath and a shiver crawls through her toes. She panics: where is his arm? She panics like a mother who misplaces a child while shopping. Where did she leave him? And who misplaces a limb? And now she has to know if the arm is under the sheet with Chester or still on the hill with the violets or at the nurse's station maybe with the cell phones and mugs in a box marked LOST AND FOUND. She tells herself, look under the sheet. So what if it's horrid. So what if she doesn't want to know how body parts come undone. She has to do it because this is a body she clung to when the hours were long and sleep far away, and car lights moved on the ceiling like comets bright for a moment, then their tails of chalk burnt out.

So she does it. She throws back the sheet and there he is. Chester with skin pale like bread dough, his arm hanging on just under the elbow by a ribbon of flesh. All the rest ripped raw, the bone sliced on the slant like cut flowers. The skin covered with lavender streaks. The scrap of a sweater cuff hangs at his wrist. A plaid sweater, though plaid isn't something Chester would wear. Linda must have picked it. Mary Lou only met Linda once at the video store. Linda whose name meant beauty, but who wasn't that because she had no chin. So the whole time Chester was explaining how Linda did this job, something with orphans and Shriners, Mary Lou kept picturing a fleet of chinless Shriner clowns in clown cars missing their bumpers, and this seemed absurd, not a thing that children should see.

And now, that dangling sweater seems silly in exactly that way. So she inches the cuff over each finger until she's holding the piece in her hand. But still something is wrong. That thread of flesh. His arm hanging on by a scrap of skin. It would have bothered him. He liked things cleanly done. He would have told her to finish the job. So she does. She rifles through her handbag until she finds scissors, the ones she carries for arts and crafts at the home. She slips her fingers into the handles and squeezes against the meaty fibers. The skin resists. So she opens the scissors wide and uses the edge of the blade to make the cut. She saws the blade back and forth until it breaks through. Then the arm falls away from the body. The pillow case slips from the pillow. Mary Lou swaddles the arm in a bundle, tucks it into her handbag, and zips it shut.

When Mary Lou opens the door, the house looks different. She's never home at this hour to see afternoon light casting a glow on dust drifting down from the doorways. In the light, the piano keys seem to shine. It's the piano Chester tuned at the nursing home a decade ago. She took it when they got a new one even though he was gone. She couldn't let it go to the curb. Mary Lou thinks she should wipe the dust from the keys, but then the telephone rings. The ringing stops, and a voice comes through the speaker. It's Sophie wondering why Mary Lou isn't at work. Saying the bingo chips are still in her car, and the ladies were looking forward to bingo, but they can't play without the chips.

In the kitchen, Mary Lou hits the delete button and erases Sophie. She kicks her shoes into a pile of sneakers and heads down the hall. In the bedroom, a towel is on the floor, still wet from the shower. The bed sheets are rumpled. A triangle of toast is stiff on the radio clock, toast with a crescent moon missing just the size of Adam's mouth. And Mary Lou thinks, shit, she's gotta get rid of Adam because Chester, in the shape that he's in, shouldn't have to deal with a boyfriend. She pulls the closet shut over Adam's dress shirts, kicks a sock under the bed. Then the toast, a beer bottle, Adam's case notes on index cards in tiny print. She shoves these things in a drawer and opens the window to air out his aftershave smell. She pulls the sheets to the headboard, something Chester would do.

How many years since he's been here? Six. No seven. She feels like she's traveled in time. It makes her body feel buoyant as she kneels on the bed, takes her handbag in her lap, and unwraps the bundle corner by corner until his arm drapes over her knee. His fingers bloom like petals. His pinkie is stiff on its hinge. Mary Lou touches his downy hair. So much like a child's arm, she thinks. The wrist thin like the head of a teaspoon. Fingernails harboring dirt.

She carries his arm to the bathroom and sets it down. She lets the water run until it is warm, puts a washcloth under the tap, rubs it with soap. Then slowly she wipes. She wipes the gash on his forearm, the yellow crust edging the jagged flesh. She teases blood clots away from the bone and rinses. The washcloth turns pink. She teases and rinses again.

How did this happen? The jagged flesh. The gash, the blood, the bone. The yellow crust like sap. The gash speckled with traces of leaves. Were there leaves on the windshield? Did he try to clear them away with his hand? No, he would have done that before he started the car. Unless he was rushed. No, Chester never hurried, she thinks.

She takes her time with his fingers. She runs the cloth over each crease, looking for clues. Over his cuticles pale and pink like earlobes. Over the scar where a wine glass broke into pieces because he was always holding things tight. Over the web of veins fanning out from wrist to knuckles. And those knuckles delicate knobs. And those fingers long and lithe. A pianist's fingers—everyone said so—they stretched the octave and had such natural curve. A pianist's fingers, but poor Chester with a brain that couldn't keep track of two sets of hands, that would focus so hard on a thumb crossing under so the pinkie could stretch up to catch the high C, that the other hand would stop mid-phrase in a gnarled pose, a clod of chords deferred.

A childhood spent at the piano. College locked in practice rooms. And at the end of it all, his playing still ruined by subtle blips and pauses, all but one song. Joplin's Maple Leaf Rag, a song already jagged and jerky. That one he could do. Of course, the career of a pianist couldn't be built on one piece. He knew his limits. For a piano tuner, one song was enough. One song to show he was more than just a mechanic. He'd bang out Joplin and piano owners would clap. Then he'd pack up his piano fingers and take them back on the road. Mary Lou wonders what he would have been if no one had told him he had the fingers of a maestro, if he had tried to be something else. She doubts they'd ever have met.

She dries his arm with a towel, finds gauze and a bandage in the back of a drawer. She holds gauze to the wound. Then around and around with the bandage, wrapping on the slant. A scalp to cover the bone. She brings his arm back to the bedroom and tucks it under the sheets on Chester's side of the bed. His fingers curl on the pillow. The bruises disappear under the blanket. She kisses his hand, and it smells like soap. She thinks of those days when a migraine sent him to bed before dinner, and she would kiss his eyelids one by one, then shut the door behind her, careful to muffle the creak. She does this now and something rises inside her, something that whispers, he's back, he's here, he's home.

By the time Adam pulls into the driveway, she's packed him a bag and left a note. Something about nursing homes and measles and spending a week with his brother—he can sleep on his couch. She packed clothes, his case notes, and a Tupperware with leftover chicken. She left the bag and note on the steps and locked the chain. Then she cleaned the house like Chester on Saturday mornings with vinegar and baking soda, an old toothbrush and a bucket of ripped up shirts. And now the house smells sweetly acidic. Baking soda splotches her arms. And she lies on the floor under the coffee table with the thick plate glass on top. She lies on a square of burgundy carpet, staring up through the glass at the ceiling fan spinning. At the stuttered blur of its blades, the pendular sway of its bulb.

She hears Adam's steps in the driveway. Then on the porch. A pause while he reads the note. The silence lingers. Then his key in the lock, the door knob turning, the clank as the door catches and holds on the chain. Then Adam's voice through the darkness. At first just a little bit worried. Lou, are you in there? Babe, unlock the chain. Then louder. Lou. Come on. This is silly. You can't have the measles. Babe, I'm tired. I'm ready for bed. Then his hand through the crack. The cuff of his sleeve. His wrist wrenches to get the chain off its track. His fingers strain further. His watch catches the lip of the door. Then the knock of an elbow. Skin scraping metal. Then, Jesus Christ damn it Lou let me in.

Adam's arm slips back into the darkness, and he presses his eye to the space between door and frame. A sliver of Adam. An eye and a nostril. The knot of his tie against his throat. He calls her again. Lou? Like a question. Lou, can you hear me? Lou, you're freaking me out. Then, Lou Lily Lou, my darling. Skip to my Lou Lou Lou. Words he sings over and over at six in the morning, loud and obnoxious, when she won't get out of bed. Then he ties all of the Lou's together and sends them into the room. Dozens of Lou's drift in the air over the glass-top table, below the whir of the fan. The Lou who plays bingo at the nursing home with Alice and Jean and Barbara. The Lou who makes chicken and dumplings Thursday nights. The Lou who buys organic eggs because Chester was always talking about cancer. The Lou who hides under a table and leaves her boyfriend's clothes on the porch. He says her name soft and it almost sounds Asian, Lu chiseled down to its basic part. Now she is *that* Lu, broken away from Mary, blending into the darkness, a bristly carpet abrading her ribs.

The phone rings, a thick electric shiver. Then Adam's voice on the speaker. Lou, I'm not leaving until you come out and say you're okay. And she knows he means it. She knows he won't walk away because what if she's hurt? What if a rapist has a knife to her neck? She crawls out from under the table and picks up the phone. I'm sorry, she says. I'm sorry I locked the door and said I was sick. And then it's just Adam and Lou on the phone. Adam and Lou and both of them breathing, inhalations crossing the line. And then because of the arm in the bedroom, she comes right out and tells him, Chester's dead, and I need some time alone. And Adam says, God, Lou, why didn't you just say so? What happened? She tells him his car went off the road. And Adam says, Are you sure you don't want me to stay? Yes, she says, but she doesn't hang up. Lou, just let me in for a second. No, she says. If you're here, I won't remember he's dead. I was a cold-hearted bitch, she says, and hangs up.

It rings again, and she leaves it. She hears him in the living room through the crack in the door. Come on, Lou. Please let me in. She doesn't answer. Okay, he says. I'll come by in the morning. Call if you need me. The door shuts and locks. She goes to the bedroom and takes off her clothes. Then she crawls under the covers and pulls Chester's arm to her breast.

When the phone rings around midnight, she's far away, her mind turning loops like an acrobat unhinged. The phone rips the softness of sleep. Then a voice fills the bedroom. A voice saying sorry to call so late. They told her she had to ask this question because Mary Lou took his wallet and keys and maybe something else. And the voice is all splinters and frayed edges. But slow. A tiptoeing voice. Cautious as it slides into the house and crosses the chasm of space to Mary Lou's bed. It's Linda. Who else could it be? Saying no she's not mad if Mary Lou took it. Though of course she's not saying she did. She's saying it's been a strange day, a god-awful day, and she doesn't know what to think. But if Mary Lou could just call back, it would be a great help. And if not, she'll come by tomorrow. Just to check if she has it. And if she does, could she give it back so they can take care of the body. At the very least, she'll come for his keys. And again she's sorry for calling so late. She'll never do it again.

The phone clicks off and Linda is gone. Mary Lou hears electricity in the wires, the thud of ice cubes at the end of the hall in the fridge. The electric hum gets louder. The sound crawls into her ears and presses against her skull. She grasps at the bed sheets looking for Chester, finds his hand and pulls it tight to her waist. She puts her hand over his and squeezes, so his fingers dig into her skin. She squeezes hard, pushing down through the muscle, clawing into the spaces between her ribs. This is where she put Chester's fingers when he couldn't calm down. When he woke in the night from that dream about a piano filled with dead birds at his conservatory audition, the judges telling him to play Chopin over and over, and Chester trying so hard to make it good. But all he got was a thud of dull notes, notes muffled by feathers. And finally the judges told him to climb into the piano and lie on that pile of bodies while someone else played Chopin pitch perfect, and the piano strings vibrated against Chester's skin.

He always had trouble sleeping. He said the world's worries marched over his face at night. He'd toss and turn, get up, and go to the bathroom. Lie on the couch. Then sit at the kitchen table. Hours later he'd crawl into bed and hold her crying. I'm tired, he'd say. I just want to sleep. His fingers would dig into her body. His knees would clutch her thighs. Always that desperate clinging. She'd say, Chester, that hurts, but he needed something to hold, so she let him and sometimes slept less than him. Those nights, she felt like a mother instead of a wife.

In the morning, Chester's arm is under her breasts. She pulls the blankets over her head and curls around him. She stares into the darkness until she sees constellations. Her breathing sounds like wing beats. The warmth of it settles on her skin. The air thickens. And she notices the air has a smell. Like sex but laced with the rot of meat.

Her fingers slip on his arm. Not the slip of perspiration, but the viscous slip of blood. She feels it on her palms. A sap seeping into the grooves of her skin. She feels it, and her pulse comes alive in her temples. She scrambles out of the sheets. She paws and scratches until his arm rips through. She looks at his arm in the light. The skin is yellow. Brown continents rise through the bandage. His nails are grey.

She wraps her robe around her, takes his arm to the kitchen. She jerks the faucet all the way up and plugs the drain. The water hisses. She implores it to spill out faster, flutters her fingers through its stream. With an inch in the basin, she sets in his arm, her hand underneath like a cradle; the other unspools the bandage and gauze. She rubs at the blood until brown threads into the water and curls around her wrist.

When his arm is clean, she empties the brine and rinses his skin. She dries him against her robe and sits on the floor to think. It's not going to work. The arm is rotting. Linda is coming. And Chester's car rolled down a hill. She tries to remember how long until the mind slips out of the body. Until cells run out of air. She considers the freezer. She could tuck him away, and it would stop the deterioration. But she can't shove him in with frozen peas and boxed lasagna and wait for his arm to cover with snow.

She thinks of something else. Under the sink is a can of polyurethane left over from the bathroom shelves. She lays wax paper over the table, cracks open the can, and stirs.

She starts at the end of the arm that once attached to an elbow, uses a pastry brush to pull syrup toward his hand. The hair glosses down in parallel ridges like matted fur. She smoothes the bubbles. Then paints another inch of skin. She spreads it thick and blows on the wet part as she paints. She lacquers over a scar from a Crock-Pot one Thanksgiving at his mother's. Dabs the bone of his wrist. Then the swirls of the knuckles. The lacquer pools in the well of his nails. One side done, she turns the arm over. Then starts at his hand and works her way up.

Maybe he was eating an apple as he drove, she thinks. And he came to the core and it was sticky on his fingers and he opened the window to toss it into a field. He would only throw something out the window if it would decompose on its own. Though she can't remember him ever snacking in the car. Or eating apples. Or hurling fruit over a lane of pavement.

The phone breaks into her thoughts. The sound vibrates in the glassy sheen of his palm. This time, after it rings and rings, a man's voice fills the room. The hospital. The balding doctor. He says they don't want to involve the police, but Mrs. Lawrence wants an investigation. Mary Lou has until noon to call. After that, they'll send an officer over. Really, they don't want it to come to that.

Of course, Mary Lou thinks. Of course, they don't want the police. She knows what they want. She goes to the bedroom and grabs yesterday's clothes from the floor, forces her limbs through the holes. She packs a duffle bag. Clothes, a toothbrush, a necklace from Adam, her mother's ring. What else? Her wallet, keys. A book. She finds the paperback she started last summer. She'll read it to Chester when they get there, wherever they go. Then the phone rings again. A swirling kind of ringing. Ringing that wraps around her knees. She crawls under the bedside table and yanks the cord. The ringing stops.

But down the hall, it rings in the kitchen still. Adam's voice tells her to pick up the phone. She follows the sound and hits the power off with her fist.

The refrigerator rumbles. The clock ticks in her scalp. She leans on the sink and looks out the window. A squirrel races across a branch with an acorn in its mouth. The acorn falls and the squirrel releases a string of angry chatter. Then a car door slams, and the squirrel clutches the tree. Mary Lou sees Linda below on the walk and drops to her knees.

She leans against the cabinets. Her pulse beats in her fingers. Her pulse beats in her teeth. Her chest heaves. She tries to swallow. Linda's hand is thudding against the door. The gasps in her chest get louder. The gasping has a rhythm. It fills her body and leaks into the cabinets behind her back. Then she closes her eyes. She's leaned against these cabinets and gasped like this before.

The last Christmas they were married, a bird crashed into the kitchen window. The house was quiet except the sound of dishes in the sink. Chester was washing and Mary Lou was eating pie when a bird thudded into the window and broke itself on the glass. A hiccup lurched from Chester's mouth, and the gravy boat fell from his fingers. It sank through the suds and split their Christmas platter in half. His eyes went from the bird caught in a string of lights in the window to the pieces under the soap.

Then something rose inside him. Mary Lou could see it climbing his neck. His chest so suddenly heaving. Gasps choking his throat. A sound like machinery seizing. Nostrils tight. Forehead covered with sweat. He grabbed her arm and squeezed, and his nails dug into her skin.

She rubbed his back. His face turned red, and his legs just crumbled. He hit the floor and heaved against his knees. And since she couldn't think what to do, she sat beside him and mimicked the wheezing. She closed her eyes and adjusted her gasps until they were perfectly timed with his. Gradually she slowed the tempo, to mute the pounding pulse, to loose the strangled lung. Until their breaths came slow together and Chester relaxed.

They leaned against the cupboards and breathed in and out to a count of three, a waltzing tempo. Chester let go of her hand and added a string of notes to the rhythm. He tapped a song on the wooden slats of the floor. His fingers leapt and jerked between the boards in pit pit patters. She put her hands over his to stop the movement, but he kept going, and her hands were pulled along. It was the closest they ever got to dancing. Like dancing on someone else's feet. And she knew he would always be scared. Music couldn't fix a thing like that.

Mary Lou hands Linda a glass of water. She sits on the couch, holding Chester's wallet and keys on her lap. She's wearing the same blouse with the silver buttons that Mary Lou bought last summer on sale. Maybe a size smaller. Maybe a thinner knit.

I'm sorry you had to come out here, Mary Lou says. I don't know why I took his things. I wasn't thinking. I should have called, but I was just so tired.

Linda sets the water on the table. Condensation drips down the glass. Linda spreads it with her thumb. She looks around the room and sniffs. Are you painting? she asks.

Mary Lou leans against the piano and looks toward the kitchen. Oh that. I polyurethaned some shelves this morning. You know, to keep my mind off things. Linda nods, slips Chester's belongings into her purse. There wasn't anything else? she asks. Anything else you took?

That's all they gave me, Mary Lou says. She stares at Linda's boots, grey suede with a lasso pattern looping around at the ankle, her feet so tiny Mary Lou imagines her wrapping them with cloth like Chinese women, each year wrapping tighter and tighter, the delicate smallness worth the crumpling of bones. Linda sees her looking, and Mary Lou asks, Are those from Macy's? Linda shakes her head no. I need to use your bathroom, she says. I'll show you, Mary Lou says, and leads her through the house. They pause in the kitchen and Linda sees the pastry brush on the table. The duffle bag on the floor. She picks the paperback up from the counter.

My aunt reads books like this, she says. Chester called it *crap lit.* Mary Lou walks past her and flips the light in the hall. The toilet's old, she says. Hold the handle down when you flush. Linda slides past. Mary Lou hears the click of the lock in the bathroom and wonders if Linda will look through the medicine cabinet. Mary Lou always does that at parties, reading the labels on pill bottles, fingering makeup and floss.

The toilet flushes. The door creaks open, and Linda's boot heels click on the hardwood floor. I should go, she says. Mary Lou offers to walk her out. She follows Linda into the living room, studying the threading on her back pockets. Her jeans look expensive, but the left leg's crooked, like she hemmed them herself. And suddenly Mary Lou wants to touch her, to put a hand on her shoulder. She doesn't want this woman to hate her. I'm sorry, she tells her. Linda nods and her chin disappears against her neck. Me too, she says. Then there's a pause.

Do you know if they found anything in the car? Mary Lou asks. Like feathers? Maybe Chester was trying to let something out when he opened the window. Maybe a bird got in. Linda cuts in, They think it was faulty brakes.

She studies the pictures on the piano. This is Adam? Mary Lou nods. Linda picks up the one behind it. A wedding, her entire family jumbled together. Mary Lou in front in a lavender dress, Chester tucked behind her in a seersucker suit. Chester had a copy of this, Linda says. I made him throw it away. She sets it behind the one of Adam and touches the piano keys. Mary Lou's pulse rises again through her ribcage and climbs her throat. Here the smell is strongest. She holds her breath.

Linda presses a few keys. I used to take lessons when I was little, she says, but I wasn't good. Not like Chester. I got him a piano last year for his birthday. He'd play in the morning, and I'd wake up to music. This morning the house was so quiet, I couldn't get out of bed. She plays with one hand, and the keys push hammers. The hammers hit strings and the strings echo, but the sound is bent. Mary Lou tells her it's out of tune. But she keeps pressing the keys, just the phrase of a song over and over. And Mary Lou listens and understands how the piano sounded in Chester's sleep, the notes knocked crooked by claws and beaks and feathers and muffled by so many wings.

Donald Anderson
  Fire Road
Dianne Benedict
  Shiny Objects
Marie-Helene Bertino
  Safe as Houses
Will Boast
  Power Ballads
David Borofka
  Hints of His Mortality
Robert Boswell
  Dancing in the Movies
Mark Brazaitis
  *The River of Lost Voices:
  Stories from Guatemala*
Jack Cady
  *The Burning and Other
  Stories*
Pat Carr
  The Women in the Mirror
Kathryn Chetkovich
  Friendly Fire
Cyrus Colter
  The Beach Umbrella
Jennine Capó Crucet
  How to Leave Hialeah
Jennifer S. Davis
  Her Kind of Want
Janet Desaulniers
  What You've Been Missing
Sharon Dilworth
  The Long White
Susan M. Dodd
  Old Wives' Tales
Merrill Feitell
  *Here Beneath
  Low-Flying Planes*
James Fetler
  Impossible Appetites

Starkey Flythe, Jr.
  Lent: The Slow Fast
Sohrab Homi Fracis
  *Ticket to Minto: Stories of
  India and America*
H. E. Francis
  The Itinerary of Beggars
Abby Frucht
  Fruit of the Month
Tereze Glück
  *May You Live in Interesting
  Times*
Ivy Goodman
  Heart Failure
Barbara Hamby
  Lester Higata's 20th Century
Ann Harleman
  Happiness
Elizabeth Harris
  The Ant Generator
Ryan Harty
  *Bring Me Your Saddest
  Arizona*
Mary Hedin
  Fly Away Home
Beth Helms
  American Wives
Jim Henry
  *Thank You for Being
  Concerned and Sensitive*
Lisa Lenzo
  Within the Lighted City
Kathryn Ma
  *All That Work and
  Still No Boys*
Renée Manfredi
  Where Love Leaves Us
Susan Onthank Mates
  The Good Doctor